Praise for the works of

Simply the Best

Karin Kallmaker has been writing romance novels for thirty years or so and she knows how to bend the rules just enough to keep things exciting…

One of the things I love in Karin Kallmaker's books is the way she sets the scene. Her characters have real jobs, not just titles mentioned here and there. It's part of who they are, part of the story, almost akin to world-building in sci-fi or fantasy. Neither fluffy nor too heavy, *Simply The Best* hits the right balance, incorporating current news and societal themes in what remains, fundamentally, a romance novel.

-*Rainbow Literary Society*

Because I Said So

Readers looking for a layered romance full of complicated feelings and a perfect ending will want to pick up this one. It might just be my favourite book from Kallmaker and it's one I'll come back to again.

-*The Lesbian Review*

Because I Said So was an incredibly fun read with some extra helpings of angst, internal and external, to elevate it to a true romance drama. Plus, I utterly enjoyed Kallmaker's mischievous play with irony when it came to the implications of the "love at first sight" experience! Sneaky!

I recommend it to fans who enjoy a richly portrayed, well-written, well-researched tale of romance with a slightly different, eccentric, exotic and an all-around fun, flavour to it! I, for one, had a blast with it!

-Bugs Cheeky, *NetGalley*

Because I Said So by Karin Kallmaker is a beautiful, though angst-filled love story. As a veteran author with some thirty books to her name, Karin is obviously skilled in writing great stories, and this book is a great example of her work.

…If you enjoy a good romance with great characters and a fair bit of angst in the story, then this book is for you.

-Betty H., *NetGalley*

My Lady Lipstick

Kallmaker fans and newcomers, both, will delight in this new tale. It has a well-written plot with innovative character drama and a love story that doesn't disappoint. The romance sparkles, the characters are enchanting, and their struggles are fascinating. Don't miss the distinctive pink cover, likely a tongue-in-cheek reference to "Anita's" grumble about her own covers! *My Lady Lipstick* is an intelligent and charming work that's sure to please.

-*Lambda Literary Review*

My Lady Lipstick is one heck of a ride and I loved every page. There were so many lovely touches that added layers to the story. I especially loved the gaming references, the baking and cooking and the depth of the characters. Both characters are expertly drawn and easy to love. I appreciated that Kallmaker made one a wonderfully complex and relatable butch. We need more butch women who are more than just one-dimensional characters. There is also something particularly special about this book. I can't quite put my finger on what it is, but there is no doubt that this is going to be one of my favourites.

-*The Lesbian Review*

Karin Kallmaker writes exceedingly good romances, and this one is a masterful mixture of a fun tale, delightful characters and her wicked sense of humour. It isn't full of laugh out loud moments, but the more subtle wit that raises a smile at the play on words and the sarcastic banter. Add in Shakespearean

character flaws along with the essential growth of our leading ladies and we have a classic. The whole is a perfectly wrapped bundle of enjoyment for anyone who likes a good romance.
-*Lesbian Reading Room*

With this two likable characters, some great secondary characters and her usual mature writing style, Kallmaker told us a very interesting story of deception, loneliness, vulnerability, broken dreams (and bones), family…and, of course, love. … *My Lady Lipstick* is a well-written story that I really liked and can easily recommend. If you have never read any of Karin Kallmaker's books (she has written nearly thirty novels; what are you waiting for!?), this one can be a good start.
-Pin's Reviews, *goodreads*

The Kiss That Counted

For years CJ Roshe has lived with the fear that "The Gathering" would find her and make her pay for turning against them. Constantly looking over her shoulder she has meticulously created a new life with no room for close friends or lovers who might ask too many questions. But her carefully constructed life begins to unravel when she falls in love with the beautiful Karita… Full of suspense and mystery, award-winning Karin Kallmaker pens another page-turner that draws the reader in with her deeply moving characters and storytelling.
-Cecilia Martin, *Lambda Book Report*

The Kiss That Counted is Kallmaker at her finest—a not to be missed romance. She offers us characters with depth and dimension, along with a rich plot, peppered with an air of mystery to keep the reader turning pages long into the night. Read it to see if CJ will be able to take control of her past and if Karita will ever be able to let down her defenses to allow someone in again. Finally, read it to see if the kiss really counted.
-Anna Furtado, *Just About Write*

Kallmaker has used the darkness of Roshe and the glow of Hanssen to tell a story filled with mystery, excitement and danger. *The Kiss That Counted* is a gripping story that will delight Kallmaker fans, and win her many more.

-R. Lynne, *Just About Write*

Love by the Numbers

First class rom-com! A wonderful witty romance and a great tale of character development and growth... The romance is sweet and the sex is hot, all in all this had my dopamine, seratonin and oxytocin levels creeping higher and higher.

-*The Lesbian Reading Room*

The love story is engaging and is filled with just the right amount of tension to make the nerve endings buzz as Nicole and Lily learn to adapt to the inevitable result of their growing passion for one another. The characters are appealing in spite of—or perhaps because of—the secrets each one holds, preventing them from opening their hearts. The story line is appealing and draws the reader in. It's also filled with that tongue-in-cheek, ever-so-sassy humor that Kallmaker does so well... Another win!

-*Lambda Literary Review*

Engrossing, Romantic and Sexy... Kallmaker's writing is so vivid—she paints the picture so wonderfully it's as if I'm right there with the characters, seeing what they are seeing, smelling the same aromas, tasting the same food. It's wonderful! I've never been to the places Nicole and Lily visit, but that doesn't matter. They are brought to life so beautifully I feel as if I have a scrapbook of my own... *Love by the Numbers* is another of Kallmaker's books that has been added to my "re-read" pile.

-*Frivolous Views*

Maybe Next Time

No "formula" romance, *Maybe Next Time* is an engrossing, compelling story of redemption, healing and surviving. Kallmaker has explored complicated themes and done so with heart and a touch of humor. In this reader's opinion, it is one of her best novels.

-Midwest Book Review

Maybe Next Time, winner of a Lambda Literary Award for Romance, has everything readers expect from a love story, but with an edge… Filled with angst, sensitivity, intimacy, and joy, *Maybe Next Time* delivers a memorable tale. With flawed but likeable main characters, an intriguing plot with many surprises, award-winning prose and flawless editing, this five-star novel epitomizes great romantic fiction. And in this reader's opinion, Karin Kallmaker tells it beautifully.

-Just About Write

Painted Moon

Painted Moon is a classic that could very well become the next *Curious Wine*.

-Lesbian Review of Books

Painted Moon has what this reader considers classic Kallmaker elements with interesting characters, wry wit and steamy love scenes. (Some of the images of Jackie and Leah have lingered in my mind for years.) If you missed this title the first time around, or if you are new to Kallmaker's novels, pick up a copy of *Painted Moon* and bask in its glow.

-Midwest Book Review

Warming Trend

Kallmaker has given us insight into human emotion along with beautiful descriptions of the Alaskan glacial terrain. *Warming Trend* will teach as well as entertain, and the broken relationship between Eve and Ani will have the reader on tenterhooks until the end.

-Anna Furtado, *Just About Write*

Kallmaker has given her fans a beautifully written novel, complete with breathtaking descriptions of Alaska. Hers is not the Alaska of the cruise lines, but the heart of Alaska, with particular attention to its glaciers, ice, and northern lights… She has told her story with great language, wit, and warmth. She's even included a very large, very lovable dog. If you're a Kallmaker fan, or if you're new to her work, *Warming Trend* is not to be missed.

-R. Lynne Watson, *Just About Write*

Substitute for Love

Kallmaker is a genius. I loved the angst, the drama and the passion… The story construction is fantastic. You get a really personal point of view from both characters. This takes a gifted storyteller, but never fear Kallmaker is here.

-*The Lesbian Review*

What would you do for someone you loved? It's easy to say you'd climb mountains and swim oceans, but when faced with a desperate choice, what would you do? That's the dilemma facing Reyna in Karin Kallmaker's newest, and I think, darkest novel… Kallmaker does a fine job exploring the anguish of Reyna's life, and the second plot, concerning a mathematician, is equally well-developed. Her major and minor characters are credible and spirited, a pleasure to meet and, sometimes, to hate. *Substitute for Love* may just be the best Kallmaker I've read in a long time, and given her extraordinary talent, that's saying something.

-Deborah Pffeifer, *Bay Area Reporter*

I've never been big on reading romance novels, which is why I'm so surprised to come to the revelation that I'm hooked on Karin Kallmaker's books... *Substitute for Love* is no exception. It doesn't seem likely for Holly, who is in a long-term straight relationship, to get involved with Reyna, who writes press releases and articles for a conservative, anti-gay Christian group, but it happens. As the story unfolds, Holly finds out some secrets about her past, while we find out the reason why Reyna has the job she has. This may be one of Karin Kallmaker's best and most engrossing books yet.

-Deborah DiRusso, *Womyn's Words*

Her plots are textured, her characters are engaging, her sex scenes are intense, and her prose style is better than workmanlike—she's the lesbian hybrid of Joyce Carol Oates (if Oates wrote briefer, less bleak books) and Danielle Steele (if Steele wrote well). *Substitute for Love* continues Kallmaker's string of darn good reads... That Kallmaker renders the tortuous travails of Holly and Reyna quite plausible is one of her novel's many charms.

-Richard LaBonte, *Book Marks*

Frosting on the Cake 3
Still Crazy After All These Years

Other Bella Books by Karin Kallmaker

When you purchase from the publisher more of your dollars reach the women who write and produce the books you love. Karin thanks you for your support of stories for and about women who love women!

18th & Castro
Above Temptation
All the Wrong Places
Because I Said So
Captain of Industry
Car Pool
Christabel
The Dawning
Embrace in Motion
Finders Keepers
Frosting on the Cake: The Original
Frosting on the Cake: Second Helpings
In Every Port
Just Like That
The Kiss that Counted
Love by the Numbers
Making Up for Lost Time
Maybe Next Time
My Lady Lipstick
Night Vision
One Degree of Separation
Painted Moon
Paperback Romance
Roller Coaster
Simply the Best
Stepping Stone
Substitute for Love
Sugar
Touchwood
Unforgettable
Warming Trend
Watermark
Wild Things

About the Author

Karin Kallmaker has been exclusively devoted to lesbian fiction since the publication of her first novel in 1989. As an author published by the storied Naiad Press, she worked with Barbara Grier and Donna McBride and has been fortunate to be mentored by a number of editors, including Katherine V. Forrest.

In addition to multiple Lambda Literary Awards, she has been featured as a Stonewall Library and Archives Distinguished Author. Other accolades include the Ann Bannon Popular Choice and other awards for her writing, as well as the selection as a Trailblazer by the Golden Crown Literary Society.

The California native is the mother of two completely grown-up, fully functional adults and blogs at her website, kallmaker.com, when the mood takes her. She adores ice cream, coffee, Tim Tams, and more ice cream. Connect with her on social media: search for "Kallmaker"—there's only one, which is probably for the best.

Frosting on the Cake 3
Still Crazy After All These Years

Karin Kallmaker

Copyright © 2025 by Karin Kallmaker

Bella Books, Inc.
P.O. Box 10543
Tallahassee, FL 32302

All rights reserved. No part of this book may be used or reproduced or transmitted in any form or manner or by any means, electronic or mechanical, including photocopying, or for the purpose of training artificial intelligence technologies or systems without permission in writing from the publisher.

This is a work of fiction. Names, characters, businesses, places, events and incidents are either the products of the author's imagination or used in a fictitious manner. Any resemblance to actual persons, living or dead, or actual events is purely coincidental. The publisher does not have any control over and does not assume any responsibility for author or third-party websites or their content.

First Edition - 2025

Editor: Medora MacDougall
Cover Designer: Sandy Knowles
Cover Author Photo: Judy Francesconi Photography

ISBN: 978-1-64247-487-9

PUBLISHER'S NOTE

The scanning, uploading, and distribution of this book via the Internet or via any other means without the permission of the publisher is illegal and punishable by law. Please purchase only authorized print or electronic editions, and do not participate in or encourage electronic piracy of copyrighted materials. Your support of the author's rights is appreciated.

Dedication

Thank you, Science. Thank you, Health Care Pros. Thank you, Firefighters. Thank you, Friends, Family, Readers, and Colleagues. We're in this together, as we always have been.

Thirty-One, Not Nearly Done

Table of Contents

To the Reader i

December: *Making Up for Lost Time* 1
    Seattle Ginger Kiss Cookies Recipe
    "Cookies and Kisses"

January: *Warming Trend/My Lady Lipstick* 19
    "Mona Lisa"

February: *Captain of Industry* 29
    "Extraordinary Thing"

March and April: *Simply the Best* 47
    "All That and a Milkshake" and "Reflections"

May: *Wild Things* 75
    "Having Faith"

June: *Painted Moon* 87
    "Living Canvas"

July: *Roller Coaster* 105
    "Heartline Roll"

August: *Maybe Next Time* 119
    "Turtles, Adagio"

September: *Above Temptation* 127
    "Kindling"

October: *Because I Said So* 143
    "The M-Word"

November: *Car Pool* 161
    "The World Heals at the Kitchen Table"

December: *Paperback Romance* 173
    "Merely Players"

And Now for the Sprinkles on Top 191

To the Reader

The stories in this third volume are presented over a calendar year and a little more for a baker's dozen of follow-ups on my novels written over the past nearly forty years. The section at the end answers many of the questions I routinely receive about the original stories. If I don't remember, I've made something up. It's a superpower.

Each story is introduced by details about the original novel, including a numbered tagline that will tell you where that novel falls in my publishing history. The information given after each story's title estimates roughly how much time has elapsed since the end of the novel to the beginning of the short story. Sometimes it's decades. Others it's a few years.

You can decide if you want to read them in the order I've chosen or start with the stories from your favorite novels. It's cake. You're a grown-up. Have your cake whenever and however you want. No one else needs to know.

–Karin

P.S. Pictures and more information about the cookie recipe can be found at my website.

MAKING UP FOR LOST TIME

Published: 1998
Characters: Jamie Onassis, master chef
                  Valkyrie Valentine, home repair expert
Setting: San Francisco and Mendocino, California

The eighth is for eternity.

Previous *Frosting on the Cake* stories:
    "Hacksaw Pastry" in *Frosting 1*.
    "Happy New Year Too" in *Frosting 2*.

Seattle Ginger Kiss Cookies

Preheat oven to 350 F. You'll need two bowls, mixer, cookie sheet(s), and a shallow dish. Bowl 2 should be suitable to use with your mixer. *Tip*: Measure dry ingredients first, then use the same cups and spoons for the wet. *Makes 60-80 cookies.*

Bowl 1 - Dry
2-1/4 cups all-purpose flour
1 tsp baking soda
1/2 tsp salt – 1 tsp if butter is unsalted
2 tsps ground ginger
1 tsp ground cardamom
3/4 tsp ground cinnamon
1/4 tsp ground clove and/or nutmeg

Bowl 2 - Wet
1/2 cup brown sugar, packed
1/2 cup white sugar
1/4 cup molasses, dark or light
1 egg or 1/4 cup nonfat liquid egg
3/4 cup chilled butter, diced

Dish - Sugar & Spice Dust
1/4 cup white sugar
1/4 tsp cardamom
1/4 tsp salt
Mix together with spoon or fork.

In Bowl 1 sift or dry whisk together all ingredients until spices are distributed.

In Bowl 2, with mixer on low, combine all ingredients except butter. Next drop in butter several cubes at a time until incorporated.

With mixer still running in Bowl 2, add 1/4 of the contents of Bowl 1, mix in, then repeat until all is mixed in. Stop mixer and scrape down sides and bottom to break up any flour clumps. Beat until all are combined.

Wash and dry hands! Test coldness of the dough by trying to form a ball by rolling dough between your palms. If any dough sticks to your hands, chill for 10 minutes. Once the dough no longer sticks to your hands, roll into 3/4" to 1 1/2" balls, and then roll each ball in the sugar dust until completely coated. (Kids love this part!)

Place balls 2" apart on parchment paper, foil, or ungreased cookie sheets.

Bake 11-13 minutes. Cookies are done when base of cookie is almost as dark as cinnamon. If using parchment or foil, lift batch immediately to a cool surface. If not, let cool completely before trying to move them.

Cool cookie sheet completely before reusing. Excellent for freezing. Smaller balls for delicate tea time trays. Larger for lunch boxes and even ice cream sandwiches.

From the Waterview Inn, Mendocino

COOKIES AND KISSES

(December, 25 Years Later)

"Holiday cookies. Doesn't matter what the holidays mean to you—it's gotta include cookies, right? Valkyrie Valentine here with your *Wednesday Wish List*. Mika L, from Vancouver, Washington, wants a quick and easy holiday cookie recipe, the kind she can make a lot of and then put in the freezer. Mika? Your wish is fulfilled with Seattle Spice Ginger Cookies. Simple to put together. With a little bit of technique, they're nearly foolproof."

Val paused to gift everyone with her megawatt smile, but Jamie had long realized it was also to take a deep breath.

Lifting first one finished cookie and then another, Val continued, "Roll them small and they're delicate on a holiday tea tray, adorable wrapped in a gift bag, and suitable all the way around the whole year, if you ask me. Practical, because you can pull them out of the freezer any time, warm gently, and they're terrific. Roll them large for chewy and soft cookies that are fantastic as ice cream sandwiches with vanilla, chocolate, or even orange sherbet as filling."

She tipped one cookie directly into the stage light. "Plus, I'm not lying—they *sparkle*. Everyone ready? As always, because we want to make sure we have all the ingredients and don't leave anything out, let's start with the *meest en*, I mean *mice en plast*—Well, shit."

Jamie tapped the recording button to stop.

Clearly annoyed with herself, Val flicked the side of her head with her forefinger. "Mumble mouth idiot." She made *bop-bop-bop* noises with her mouth followed by a motorboat bilabial fricative and finished off with exaggerated smoochie lips accompanied by a drawn-out repetitions of *kewww*.

Jamie was unsuccessful smothering her laugh. She weathered Val's annoyed look with a sunny one of her own. "You want me to stop when you flub, right?"

"Yes. I'll go back to a good spot and start over from there. When Abshir gets back, she'll splice the takes together. I want to get the recording over with so I can cover the herb garden before the next storm."

December weather in Mendocino was so often foggy and wet that Jamie was cheered by the thought of spring. "I'm looking forward to the fresh basil already."

"Bring me pesto-avocado toast in bed?"

Jamie's mouth was already watering at the thought and not entirely because of the food. "You know I will."

"Oh, and a countdown at the top—don't say 'action.'"

Everything Jamie knew about being behind the cameras came from watching the technologically savvy Abshir work with Val. Feeling self-conscious, she kept one finger on the Record button and used her other hand to indicate five. "Okay, five, four…" with her hand counting down. She mouthed, "three," pressed the red button, and continued the countdown with just her hand. At the silent zero she pointed at Val.

Val launched again into the introduction while Jamie's gaze darted between Abshir's laptop screen and the four monitors that showed the four camera feeds. The laptop screen was an array of pulsating meters and controls she'd been told to NEVER EVER touch, with the exception of the video recording button.

Abshir had left her usual meticulous instructions, and Jamie hoped to prove herself not the hopeless tech noob she undoubtedly was. Val's home studio bristled with all the cameras and lights it took for her to film the forty episodes a year of her television show *Simplicity* to meet Warnell Communications standards for broadcast.

While running the Waterview Inn and keeping it a strong part of their small-town community, Jamie had followed the massive shifts in the media landscape that had affected Val. A couple of decades ago, she'd started as a writer for a home and garden magazine, then moved in front of the camera with a regularly scheduled Sunday night hour-long do-it-yourself remodel show called *A Month of Sundays*. The magazine had faded away, taking with it Val's column that combined recipes, repairs, and home decor projects. Val's pivot had been to *Simplicity*. What she used to write she now performed as a half-hour weekday show.

It had been a huge success. Jamie was on the show's credits as Food Consultant—and seeing it never failed to give her a little thrill. When Warnell had syndicated *Simplicity* outside the US markets, Val had used the extra money to build a home studio so she could film *Simplicity* without being away for weeks at a time.

At first, running the tech side of the studio had been simple. Raw footage was sent to Warnell producers who used the same personnel as always to cut and fit the footage to its time slot. But over the years, as magazine and broadcast revenues plummeted, Warnell had changed up their agreements with content producers like Val. Instead of the hired front-end face of a show Warnell produced, they wanted independent creations that came to them finished.

That meant another pivot—Val had become her own producer.

The pandemic changed everything again. *A Month of Sundays* couldn't be produced because of the travel and contact, and Warnell had no interest in ordering more episodes even though people were eager to spend their spare time on renovations. They still wanted *Simplicity*, but who knew for how long?

On top of that uncertainty, all the messaging they sent Val about audience metrics was focused on competing with social media and grabbing youth attention. While Val could tok a tik with the best of them, at nearly sixty she was one of Warnell's oldest on-air talents. Val—ever a realist—saw the handwriting on the wall. Warnell Media could drop her completely, so she needed to invest in her own brand and name recognition beyond television. Hence, the casual *Wednesday Wish List* videos and livestreams that belonged entirely to Valkyrie Valentine.

Through all of the change, Val had been able to hire remote contractors to edit and generate the projects meant for Warnell's broadcast. The hard part had been finding someone to be in-studio for the more casual recordings. Abshir, who lived a few miles north in Fort Bragg with her family, had mad skills with tech and was the answer to Val's prayers. This week, however, Abshir was in Mecca with her grandfather to complete Umrah. That left the tech side to Jamie.

"Hit Record and touch nothing else," Abshir had said. "Once to turn on, once again to turn off."

"It'll be easy," Val had assured her.

Nerve-wracking was what it was. Jamie could taste and identify four different peppers in a broth, but when Abshir had arrived for her initial interview and asked if she could adjust a focus-directional-thingy-whatever, both she and Val had gone "Ooo" at the result that looked one million percent the same to Jamie.

Takes all kinds, Jamie reminded herself. Val went "Ooo" over the difference between Belgian and Venezuelan cocoa the same way Jamie did. When asked the secret of their long relationship, Jamie always said, "We like the same chocolate."

Though she had Jamie stop recording a couple more times, Val hit her stride when it came to making her usual salt-and-pepper-wavy-hair-bright-flawless-skin-flirty-eye-sexy-flannel-shirt-competence-come-to-momma love to the camera. Jamie still didn't know how Val made that kind of magic, but she was grateful every day that the charm was all hers to enjoy in person.

"Okay, let's pause, and I'll do a little clean up and get ready to sample and plate. You could join me for that bit, if you want."

"I am *not* camera ready." Jamie gestured at the dried stain from sloshed marinara sauce from the lunch service. The Waterview kitchen was closed for dinner in the off-season except Fridays and Saturdays, and that had given Jamie the freedom to cover Val's Wednesday afternoon recording session. She would be very grateful to leave all the tech to Abshir next week for the biweekly livestream event.

"Fine." Val pouted at her. "I'll finish up then."

"Five, four…" Jamie pressed Record again, pointed at Val, and rested back on the chair to watch her adorable wife take a sizable bite of the cookie and melt over the taste. It wasn't an act—Jamie had helped fine-tune the recipe and the chewy cookies with a little crunch at the edges and sugar topping were flat-out addictive.

"Thanks for joining me this week," Val said to the camera. She took another bite from the cookie in her hand. In a cookie-crumb voice she continued, "Sorry, they're so good I can't help myself. Next week I'll post a demo for quick and affordable guest room fixes for those of you expecting overnight visitors this holiday season."

After about three seconds of holding her stage smile, Val relaxed. "And we're out. Thank you, honey. I couldn't have done it without you."

Jamie made her way around the long table where Abshir had carefully arranged the equipment. Stepping over the color-coded cables taped carefully to the floor, she joined Val behind the staged kitchen counter. It was on wheels, presently locked, so it could be rolled to one side in favor of Val's demonstration workbench or the crafting table. Leaning against it, she eyed the platter of sparkly copper-hued ginger cookies. The aroma of cinnamon and cardamom, so warm and gently sweet, reminded her that lunch had been a couple of hours ago. "Am I going to be paid in cookies?"

"Well, if all you want is cookies, okay."

Jamie promptly helped herself to one nearest to her. It was no longer warm, but that hardly mattered. She'd swallowed a second chewy, spicy bite before she brushed a crumb off her lips and asked, "What else could I get?"

Val blinked far too innocently. "Use your imagination."

"I'm going to get that anyway. Later. But I'd definitely take a kiss right now."

"That is actually what I had in mind. You're clearly the gutter-brain in this relationship."

"And who might I have learned that from?"

Val wrapped her long arms around Jamie's waist. Up close the layer of stage makeup and heavy eyeliner was more apparent. Jamie had gotten used to it, but she still struggled at times, feeling like dowdy vanilla next to vibrant saffron.

Val nuzzled her ear. "If you're insinuating that I've corrupted you, I'm going to remind you of who painted who with chocolate all those years ago."

Jamie arched her neck in response to the warmth of Val's lips. "I am not responsible for my actions when you wear a tool belt."

Laughing, Val kissed Jamie lightly and followed it with a deeper kiss filled with memories of all the kisses that had come before this one.

She sighed when their lips parted. "How do you take my breath away every time you do that?"

"Scoot up onto the counter and I'll demonstrate again."

"Why, Ms. Valentine, how you do talk." Jamie complied and spread her knees so Val could stand between them. Upstairs there were no sauces on the cooktop or cakes in the oven. There was time for kisses. Time to enjoy the warmth in Val's deep violet-blue eyes.

"Talking isn't what I have in mind."

She cupped Val's face. "I love you."

Val's soft sigh was Jamie's favorite music. Their lips met again, this time opening to each other for familiar, intimate exploration. Val tasted of ginger and cardamom—Jamie supposed she did too. Her senses were filled up in the very best way.

She was delightfully unsure how much time had passed. All she knew was that Val's hands had slid under her shirt to massage her lower back.

She was considering perhaps unbuttoning Val's shirt when Val murmured, "We're burning through the electric bill leaving these lights on."

"I suppose." She pushed Val back. "I'll see you later."

"You can count on that, you sexy thing." Val made her way to the tech table and the studio lights went out. "What's for dinner?"

Jamie blinked in the abrupt dimness. "I've got chicken cacciatore to heat up and fresh broccoli."

Val wrinkled her nose. "Broccoli? Do we have to?"

"Broccoli is the price we pay for chocolate cake."

"There's chocolate cake?"

"Maybe." Jamie waggled her eyebrows.

Val kissed the side of Jamie's mouth, then brushed her lips along the curve of Jamie's earlobe. "There are always the best kinds of rewards for your chocolate cake."

"In that case, let me shut off the laptop and we can get the broccoli out of the way." Abshir had been adamant that all Jamie had to do now was close the laptop, and so that's what she did.

* * *

Val swept back the curtains to let in the bright light of a rare sunny December morning for coastal northern California. She knew from the buttery, succulent aroma of tomato and spinach omelets wafting up to their third-floor suite that Jamie was already in the inn's kitchen feeding the paying B&B guests and locals.

"Heaven on earth," she murmured as she let the sun warm her face. Mostly it was because Jamie was here. But not only that.

Last night, with Jamie's satisfied breathing under Val's ear, she'd had a moment of grumpiness. Nearly sixty and having to reinvent herself all over again. She enjoyed the video and livestreams. She hadn't knocked down a wall in far too long, though.

She ought to have fallen happily asleep, grateful that all of her body still worked, for the most part, and that Jamie's body still appreciated some particular moves after all these years. But instead of embracing contentment and happy snores, she had lain awake wondering why the renewal order for more episodes of *Simplicity* hadn't yet been signed.

It's just business, she'd tried to tell herself, but it was also her life. She might have worried awake all night, but Jamie had snortle-snored, and it still made Val laugh. The tension had broken and finally, she'd slept.

Overslept, even.

After a quick shower to rinse away all the smells that had been so sexy the night before, she pulled on work jeans and a boxy blue sweatshirt. Tired of the blowout mane she wore for the camera, she tied it all back in a ponytail. She'd promised Liesel she'd walk over the two blocks to see if she could figure out why the burners on her stove had stopped working. Even in her seventies, Liesel was independent, but she confessed the issue had her stumped.

As she skipped down the stairs, she checked her phone. It was a banner day for hackers, it seemed, as three people on her trust list had forwarded a video with the caption "IS THIS YOU?" She knew better than to click on the link.

She dropped a kiss on the back of Jamie's neck on her way to the toaster. Six slices of sourdough bread from a bakery in Fort Bragg had popped up as if volunteering to be part of her breakfast. She forked them onto the cookie sheet where Jamie would add them to plates.

"Two of those slices are yours," Jamie informed her.

"You are such a good woman. You want one?"

"I've already had breakfast."

"That doesn't answer my question."

Jamie's quiet laugh was pleasing. "Yes, I want one."

"Jam?"

"What do you think?"

"Jam it is."

Jamie's hands were busy with one of the sauté pans, so Val held out the slathered toast for Jamie to take a bite. Some of the peach jam got on her creamy cheek. It was not unattractive.

"Whoops! I'll take care of that." Val swooped in to lick it clean.

"I think you did that on purpose."

"How could you think such a thing?"

"It's not like we just met." Jamie scattered a pinch of dried herbs on the contents of the pan.

"I swear if I knew how to sing I'd be belting out 'Oh, What a Beautiful Morning' on my way to Liesel's."

"It is rather glorious out there, isn't it?"

"After a glorious night."

Jamie looked smug. "It was, wasn't it? Here, flip this for me. I need two things from the walk-in."

Potatoes O'Jamie, it looked like. Cubed Yukon Golds that had been sprayed with olive oil and roasted, then sautéed with thinly sliced mushrooms and caramelized onions. *Come to mama*, Val thought. "Did you already salt these?" she called out.

"No," came the clear reply. As Jamie emerged from the walk-in refrigerator, bag of baby spinach and block of cheese in hand, the Inn's phone rang. Jamie lifted the handset to her ear and said in a cheerful voice, "Thank you for calling the Waterview. How can I—oh hi, Liesel."

"Tell her I'll be there in about ten minutes," Val suggested.

"Val will be—what do you mean I'm on the Internet?"

Focused on her task, Val slid the golden, sizzling potatoes out of the skillet and into their chafing dish and lightly salted them.

Jamie whirled around to gape at Val. "What do you mean I'm on the Internet kissing Val? Oh. My. God. Do we—do we talk about broccoli and chocolate cake?"

Oh no. Val wiped her hands and fished her phone out of her back pocket. A couple of taps later she opened one of the emails she'd thought was a hacker video and read the whole message.

The production assistant at Warnell had added below the URL, "Val, this was accidental, right?"

They hadn't been only recording last night.

They'd also been *livestreaming*. All the flubs and her occasional cussing would have been broadcast to the fan club, and of course many fans would have tuned in after they got a notification that a broadcast had started. They saw all the flubs…and Jamie.

Kissing and sexy foreplay talk with Jamie.

What exactly did we say?

Jamie disconnected the call with an agonized gasp. "What did I do wrong? I did what the instructions said. At least I tried to."

Val took a deep breath. "Okay, this is embarrassing—"

"Oh, you think so?" Jamie asked with mock incredulity.

"—But if I remember what we said, it was mostly lovey-dovey. And thank goodness we agreed that beds are more comfortable than countertops."

Jamie clapped a hand over her mouth as her face crimsoned.

Val thumbed open her phone and tapped the preset to search for her name in social media over the last twenty-four hours. "Hey, hey, well, we're an adorable lesbian couple caught smooching in the kitchen. Foodie TikTok is using *CookiesandKisses* as the hashtag."

She scrolled down the results. Some of the headlines and tags were more graphic. "Let's see. 'Val Valentine fans get a behind-the-scenes eyeful.' This one's cute—'No lesbian bed death here!' A bunch of 'Sapphic Snogging.' And there's 'Sexy talk sizzles in boo-boo lesbionic video.'" She stuck her tongue out at the phone. "Ugh—*lesbionic*? Who says that these days?"

Jamie uncovered her mouth to let words out all in the tumble. "What is Warnell going—what will they think? It wasn't on purpose—I didn't know what I was—could this endanger your contract for *Simplicity*?"

"The whole world knows we're a couple. Okay, here's someone who thinks it was a clever marketing ploy, not a mistake, but there's nothing in it that's bad for the Warnell brand. Or mine. Quite the contrary—and the shares and views are going through the roof. Okay, this stitch is kind of ouch. 'Seniors sexy talk gives us all hope.' *Seniors?* Maybe, I guess." She flicked the screen to see more views. "I thought Sixty was the New Forty, but whatever. Wanna watch it?"

Jamie shook her head vehemently. "If I don't watch it, then I can pretend people don't know how we kiss."

She flashed her phone at Jamie. "This influencer thinks we're a great how-to for chemistry."

"I don't think this is as funny as you think it is."

Finally taking full notice of Jamie's storm-cloud face, Val said, more seriously, "I'm super glad we remained clothed."

"My hair was a mess, and my mouth was full of cookies."

Val wanted to add, "And my tongue," but thought better of it. Jamie had never yearned for the spotlight. She was probably going to be the person most upset by the gaffe. Not that Val was happy her fans had discovered how often she said "shit" when things went wrong.

Her cell phone rang. She took one look at the name and braced herself. "It'll be okay," she said to Jamie before she accepted the call.

* * *

Sure, Val thought this was all so funny. Had the marinara on her shirt been visible? Had she said aloud any of the words that had been running through her head as Val kissed her?

Val was saying, in her most silky voice, "Why hello, Sheila. How is the CEO of Warnell Media doing this fine morning?"

Ugh. Sheila Thintowski. Jamie had never liked the woman. When she'd taken over Warnell from her father, the mood of the company had shifted—or at least it seemed to Jamie. Maybe it *was* simply market forces and not Sheila's doing. Still.

"Of course it was an accident. It's looking like a happy accident, isn't it? I think the settings from the last session were still in place, which was a livestream, and it didn't get updated when we recorded yesterday." Val seemed to be choosing her words carefully. "I did it without my usual technician and didn't check the settings. My bad."

Jamie took a deep breath. It was Val to the core to take responsibility. Maybe it was possible some setting had been left on—it did let her off the hook for the massive flub.

How am I going to face anyone? Liesel had seemed shocked. She'd also laughed, but the shock was there. Of course Liesel had spent too much of her life closeted in the military, and public displays of ardent affection were not something she was entirely comfortable with.

Sheila's tone seemed highly excited, but what else was new? Jamie couldn't make out the words.

Val hmphed. "It only went out to *Wednesday Wish List* subscribers, but someone must have captured it."

She was going to spend the rest of her life wondering who'd seen it and if any odd looks she got were because of ginger cookies and long, languid kisses.

"That's probably best. Don't engage directly. It'll blow over, and nobody seems very shocked. They see much more revealing accidents on any social media platform."

Sheila said something emphatic, but Val cut her off. "I know TikTok has a quick shelf life, but it's trending on Insta too. Facebook attention can drag out for days. There'll be people who don't see it until next week. This kind of thing will have a long, long tail. Wait until queer media gets a hold of it."

More tinny voice.

Jamie shook herself out of her shock and plated the potatoes with the omelet and carried it from the kitchen out to the local who stopped in several times a week. She'd turned on the dining room's center fireplace to shake off the morning chill, and the handful of diners had settled near it. It had seemed as if the morning would be a calm one—lazy even.

She stifled a groan.

Len, his gray hair in its usual wild tangle, was watching something on his phone but quickly put it down as Jamie approached.

Crap-on-a-biscuit. She set the plate in front of him, saying, "Potatoes extra crispy the way you like."

"Thanks." He wouldn't quite meet her eyes.

"Anything interesting on the web today?"

"Uh—"

"You saw the video."

"Yeah. I always watch Val. She's our local girl made good. Yes, uh, it was really interesting." He added hurriedly, "Interesting the way she'd stop when she made a mistake and start over."

Val would be pleased to hear that she was considered a local girl. It had only taken twenty-five years. "It was supposed to be edited before anyone saw it."

"Of course." After an awkward pause, Len added, "Those cookies surely did look good."

"I'll tell Val you thought so."

She held her head up until she was safely past the kitchen door. She banged her head against the nearest cupboard. *Oh. My. God.*

Val, silkier than ever, was saying, "I've got reach into multiple demographics, and this proves it. So get the Home and Garden Digital exec to send me the renewal contract for *Simplicity* already. I agreed to the terms three weeks ago."

Jamie kept walking until the walk-in freezer door was closed behind her. She'd always liked the cold for a minute or two—it was very focusing.

It had been perhaps three minutes before the door opened. "You don't need to hide. It's not a scandal."

"The customers will all see it."

"Not all."

"But I won't know who."

"You don't know who's read your cookbooks either, and it's kind of the same thing, isn't it?" Val held out her hand. "I'm sorry it happened, sweetie. But it's fine."

Jamie left the chilled air of the freezer and warmed her hands on the front of the oven.

"Sheila *said* she was going to make sure I got the *Simplicity* renewal. That way they can ignore the Cookie Incident, as she called it, and bury it with a renewal announcement."

"So maybe it was a good thing?"

"There's no maybe about it." Val lifted Jamie's hands to her face. "However it happened, a little bit of viral video is good for me." She kissed Jamie's fingertips, then pulled her close for a smooch.

"Lord, they're going at it again!"

Jamie sprang back with a gasp. "Jeff O'Rhuan! Wipe that smirk off your face or there's no coffee for you."

Her old high school mate and long-time fresh fish supplier did not wipe his knowing smirk off his face as he helped himself to a steaming cup. "My dad said it did his heart good, seeing old married people carrying on for once."

At the same time Val exclaimed, "Old?" Jamie protested, "Carrying on?"

"You got another word for it?"

Val opened her mouth, but Jamie forestalled her with, "No comment. I have no comment now and never will."

"And here I was hoping you'd be making a batch of those Ginger Kiss Cookies."

"They're not called Ginger Kiss…" Val's voice trailed away.

Jamie rolled her eyes. "This is never going to blow over if you keep reminding people about it."

Val batted her eyelashes and gazed at Jamie through them. When Jamie continued to glare, she added puppy-whimper noises.

She was not going to give in to Val's adorableness. "It's not funny, Val. I'm not the public person you are."

"I know, sweetheart, but we can't put the genie back in the bottle. Cat's out of the bag. The dough has risen. The lumber's cut." She fluttered her eyelashes again.

Dang it—it was unfair how cute Val could be when she wanted. "And I should make the best of it?"

"Well, yes. You could put the recipe on the Inn's website, cross out the old name, and handwrite in the new one. Wait for it to be discovered, and a whole lot of people will visit the site. Where they can also order signed Waterview cookbooks and merch."

Jamie glowered. Next thing Val would want to add aprons that blazed forth LESBIAN KISSING HERE and they'd sell like hotcakes.

Val gestured like a magician manifesting gold. "Lemon meet lemonade."

"There are things about the world I don't care for," Jamie muttered. There was at least one shop in town that would stock aprons like that. *Dang it, I'm turning into Val.* Which maybe wasn't a bad thing, given how much she loved and respected Val. "But I guess this won't be one of them."

A throat was cleared behind them. "Might we order our breakfast?"

Jamie whirled to see one of the overnight guests lingering hopefully in the kitchen doorway. "Of course. I'm so sorry. A little distracted this morning." Jamie ushered the guest back to the table where his husband was already seated.

"Understandable. You two, by the way, are *adorable*. We watched the whole thing twice."

The waiting husband almost bounced in his seat. "I'm going to make those kissy cookies the moment we get home. I mean, if they're really that good."

"They really are. We've got some left from the demo—I'll bring you a couple. Val and I worked on the recipe together. The cardamom in the sugar dust was her idea, though. Pure genius."

She talked through what they wanted for breakfast and returned to the kitchen to start on a tomato frittata for two with a dish of olive tapenade on the side, slices of toast, and a shared slice of breakfast pie after, with coffee. When traffic was as slow as it always was in early December, she preferred being a short order cook for quick, fresh, and delicious basics to masterminding daily menus.

Jeff O'Rhuan had departed. Val was whisking eggs. "I heard the word frittata."

"Five eggs, herbs—"

"And a dollop of milk, dash of white pepper, no salt until it's done, yes, I know. Is this your last order for the morning?"

"Yes."

"Why don't I help you clear up and we'll go over to Liesel's together and see to her pesky stove." Her tone was a little wistful as she added, "It's a beautiful morning out there. I'd love to spend it with you and forget all about the Internet."

Jamie was pushing the frittata pan under the broiler when she said, "It's not that I'm embarrassed that people know how much I love you, you know."

"Honey, I didn't think that was it, not even for a moment."

She set the timer for a minute and forty-five seconds.

Val opened the hot water tap over the wash sink.

One minute and forty seconds.

Jamie sidled up behind Val and reached around her to turn off the water. "We could do dishes, I suppose."

She felt Val laugh. "Or?"

"One minute and thirty-five seconds of making out on the back stairs."

Val snuggled Jamie's arms even tighter around her, and they shuffle-walked in tandem out of sight of any of the guests.

Just as Val's lips were about to touch hers, Jamie murmured, "Good lord..."

"They're at it again," Val finished.

WARMING TREND

Published:	2009
Characters:	Anidyr Bycall, doctoral candidate (glaciers) and bartender
	Eve Cambra, restaurateur
	Tan Salek, college administrator
	Lisa Garettson, cocktail waitress
Setting:	Key West, Florida, and Fairbanks, Alaska

Twenty-One! Finally of Age, Finally Legal

Previous *Frosting on the Cake* stories:
"Good Morning" in *Frosting 2*

MY LADY LIPSTICK

Published:	2018
Characters:	Paris Ellison, romance writer, video game designer
	Diana Beckinsale, reverse tomb raider
	Lisa Garettson, owner of the Mona Lisa bar
Setting:	Boston, Massachusetts, and County Kent, England

Twenty-Eight, the Same Number as My Age when I Completed My First Novel
Or a Perfect Cribbage Score, Sans a One-Eyed Jack

MONA LISA

(January, 16 and 7 Years Later)

Let me tell you about The Cold.

Years ago I surfed and I partied. I brought the keg to the beach more than once. Have you ever carried a chilled keg out to a beach? Had your arms and shoulders get red and stiff all the way to the bone, and it took an hour for the sun to melt them back to normal?

Or taken a hefty swallow of vodka that just came out of the freezer? Your throat burns and freezes at the same time, and it's hard to breathe for a couple of seconds?

That's all *wimpy* cold. Nothing to do with real cold.

Real cold is Fairbanks, Alaska.

It's been -40 Fahrenheit for ten days. For nine days the sign on the front door of the Mona Lisa Boston Pub has been turned to "Closed for The Cold." Regular customers know what that means. The tourists should stay inside their hotels anyway.

Go outside, can't breathe. Inside it's like you're wrapped in ice. The only place that's warm is bed.

As far as I'm concerned, this demonstrates the magic of nature, because the sun sets at three p.m. and won't come up for twenty hours. Clearly, Mother Nature wants us to have sex. My wife, Tan, is agreeable to this way of looking at the situation.

Surprise revelation for me: you can't spend all the awake time you're in bed having sex. We have tried. That was the first four nights.

Tonight's night five and we've decided on an audiobook mystery. And we don't love each other one tiny bit less. If anything, we love each other even more. I look at her perfect brown skin, dark eyes, round cheeks, and smooth black hair that's cut short enough to show off her neck and collarbone—I look any hour of the day or night and a little bit of my heart stops in awe of how strong, handsome, and so very delicious she is.

Best part? If she catches me looking, I see the exact same feelings in her eyes. It still amazes me that she loves me, because at first I thought she thought I was a bubblehead. I know for a fact that my BFF, Ani, told her something along the lines of, "Lisa is annoying," because Ani is stubborn and won't admit that 99.9 percent of the time I'm right about, well, everything.

Like yesterday, in Eve's cafe down in North Pole, where we played *Settlers of Catan* and huddled over coffee and tea all day for warmth, I told Ani that Eve had been cooking all morning and likely needed a little bit of a break and maybe she ought to go kiss her, you know, perk up the day.

Ani: I can't do that here.

Me: Whyever not? Everybody knows you're a couple.

Ani: It'll embarrass her.

Me: You mean it'll embarrass you. Who has wood for my sheep?

Ani: This is her place of business.

Me: She's been businessing all morning. Show her some love.

Ani: When I want to.

Tan: I would take your sheep for grain. Ani, it sounds like you don't want to now.

Ani: I'd have thought of it on my own.

(She sounds like a mule. I have told her about this, and yet here we are.)

Me: In which case, why are you being so resistant? Because I said it first?

And then I'm rolling my eyes, and she's scrunching her face in unattractive ways.

Seriously, we go through this *every* time. Tan says that Ani and I exasperate each other so easily because we knew who we each were the moment we met. I guess that's true. I tried to get Ani to give me an extra share of her tips when we were both working at the ice bar in Key West—that was before the big mystery and reconciliation between her and Eve.

Which I solved, for the record. Ani forgets this.

Anyway, the night we met I tried all my best moves and got zilch in response.

Okay, I get it that I have a curvy shape and the big blue eyes that society has decided are desirable traits. I was born this way, and I will use all the tools I got at birth when necessary. That includes my brain, and I don't suffer from too much guilt when my brain wins out over someone who presumes my boobs mean I don't even have one.

Ani, super sexy in fingerless gloves, threw me big side-eye the moment we met, so I guess Tan is right. We knew each other's bullshit at minute one, and you keep a friend like that. Especially if she spends all her life making her life harder than it should be—the woman needs me.

She seemed to be an ice queen, and I mean that literally because she's got degrees and super smarts in glaciers and cold frozen things. She starts conversations with, "The Ruth Glacier is losing three feet every year now. The Naomi is almost as bad."

Which is alarming, I get that. Best as I understand it, that three feet off the glacier that fills one of the deepest gorges on the entire planet drains into the ocean and eventually becomes hurricanes. So that's not good.

Anyway, she tried to lie to me about being over Eve, but duh. I made her comb her hair at least. Yes, I had to tell her to do this, and to put on a fresh shirt, before bursting in on Eve after years. Seriously, if I was going to show up on my ex's doorstep would I deliberately want to look like something a cat wouldn't even drag in?

Oh, so yeah, case in point. I finally get wood for my sheep and build a settlement while Ani goes and nuzzles Eve's neck, and then there's a smooch, and then they disappear into the storeroom for a couple of minutes, and then they both looked warmer, happier, and pleased.

Did I get any thanks? No, I did not.

Typical.

Tan fell asleep during Chapter Three of our mystery, and the remote is all the way over on her nightstand. I don't want to move to pause the playback because she could roll over, and right now her strong face is burrowed against my thigh. I'll let my thigh turn into stone before I'll risk waking her.

The letter that had arrived earlier from Paris is within reach on my bedside table. Paris Ellison, my dear friend and someone who knew right away that taking my advice worked out, is one-half of the writer known as Anita Topaz. Maybe you read *Hands off the Merchandise* or saw the movie streaming? The other half is her wife, Diana Beckinsale. They met in my bar in Boston, back when Tan had taken a job in administration at the University of Massachusetts. We were there nearly eight years, and then the uni here in Fairbanks wanted her back, and of course I said yes because Tan missed her family.

Also, I didn't yet have a clear understanding of The Cold.

I made a hell of a profit on my bar in Boston too and invested it building a Boston-style pub in Fairbanks. The new bar is named Mona Lisa, after the one in Boston, which I bought in part because its neighborhood-famous name was in fact my middle name, Lisa. Nobody wants to go to a bar called "Myra's" and nobody calls me by my first name either. Not more than once.

Anyway, my bar is where Diana and Paris met. Only Diana wasn't Diana at the time. She was going by Fiona. I *knew* something wasn't quite right about her. Maybe it was because she was utterly and completely *exactly* who she appeared to be. Nobody is that square on.

Paris figured it out before I did. In my book, that makes Paris one of the smartest people I know.

I'd read the letter the moment I got back inside after the walk to the mailbox. By the way, all my thanks and praise to postal workers this time of year.

Along with the news from County Kent all the way in England, where Paris and Diana spend half the year, Paris had written that Diana was pregnant.

I'm thrilled for them. Diana wasn't sure it could happen—long story—but it did after a couple of tries with a medical grade turkey baster process. Paris also wrote how anxious she was about becoming a mom, which is very Paris. I'll remind her when I write back that she had a really great mom, may she rest in peace, and, apparently, Diana's mom is terrific, so there's that in their favor. They'd had good examples, which is more than I can say for myself.

They're both imaginative people, which I have to think would be great for raising a little human being. Plus Diana is fearless. Another long story, but Paris said if she told me about Diana's side gig, I wouldn't believe her, which is possible. Paris does make up stuff for a living.

Tan's breathing is deep and steady, soothing and adorable. That is, I usually find it soothing, but I'm also hearing the clock on the dresser ticking and tocking away the seconds, minutes, and hours.

And I'm thinking what I really hear is the ticking of my biological clock and wondering if I've waited too late to realize maybe I do want to squeeze a small human being out into the world. Or catch one Tan squeezed out. Or adopt. Or all of the above, I don't know, I just think…

I know all the way deep down that Tan would be a terrific mother. She asked once, maybe ten years ago, if I'd thought about it. I had laughed. I'd said no, I'm not the maternal type.

She's never brought it up again, and now I'm thinking I should have heard her out.

Ani says all the time that I'm selfish. Ani's full of it, but maybe this time I had been a little bit selfish, and I certainly wasn't going to tell Ani about it.

Wrapped up in bed, surrounded by the warmth and smell of Tan, I've never felt such peace. There's the bliss of sex, which I really like, and then there's this—this—what would be the right word? Safety? Balance? Comfort? It's a lot like that feeling when the sun finally melts your shoulder that was frozen by the keg you carried out to the beach. So deep that all that's left is peace.

I've been on my own since I was fifteen. Made a lot of mistakes early on. Fewer as I got older, which I guess is a reason to get older. Mostly though, loving and being with Tan like this wasn't something I expected. I'd never seen how love changed people until it changed me, I guess.

For example, I am being philosophical, which is totally new to me. I'm thinking maybe I never thought I could be a decent parent because mine were such a crapshow.

It's starting to feel like I did to myself what I have said other people did to me all my life. I saw the reflection of myself in Tan's eyes and thought, "That girl? No way is she the mothering type."

If we are going to do something about it, it has to be soon. My eggs aren't getting any younger. Tan's are a bit younger than mine, and, you know, I think I'm going to cry.

Because I bet Tan has *perfect* eggs, and she has a large, boisterous family like I never did, and I think maybe I stomped on her hope of a family because I was busy limiting myself to a person I'm not anymore. We are already a family, I know that, but maybe there's a different meaning to that word, and she'd like to have that, but accepted my decision without question because she loves me.

I mean, who does that? She does, that's who.

I'm not worthy. And she's so lucky to have me.

And I think maybe both can be true?

I will not wake her up and ask. That would pile on the selfishness. Yet it's no surprise that her eyes are open now.

"What are you crying about, honey? What did I do?"

"You didn't do anything. You're perfect, you know."

One hand came out from under the covers to grapple for the stereo remote. The audiobook playback stops. "You're never wrong, so I guess I'm perfect. What's making you sad?"

"Do you want to have a family?"

She blinks at me. "How do you mean?"

I hate it when I can't tell what she's thinking. "A kid. Kids."

"What brought this on? That Diana's pregnant?"

"I was thinking about that, yes, and then I remembered you asked once. I didn't give you a chance to ask again, did I?"

She kisses my thigh, the bit of me closest to her mouth. "I've got a sister and cousins who had kids before they were ready and with partners who were really not ready. It was rough on everyone. You didn't seem ready, and I didn't want to do it without you."

"But you'd like to?"

She wiggles a little more upright. Lord, her body is warm against mine. "I'd like to talk about it. If you want to."

I nod, swallowing hard.

With a graceful twist she snags a tissue off the bedside table. "Thank you for bringing it up."

"I'm afraid I won't be a good mom."

She snaps upright. "Why on earth would you think that?"

"My mom—"

"Babe, are you serious? You aren't her. You are the mother of your entire world. Me. Ani."

"Ani really needs it."

"I know, maybe not as much as you think she does, but she does tend to pick the hard way most of the time."

I shrug at the truth of it.

"But, honey, you mother every single person who comes into the bar. You don't just hand out excellent advice. You have an amazing gift for getting people to do things for other people. Like changing a flat tire."

"Oh, that's easy. I just ask."

Tan's velvety brown eyes roll heavenward for a moment. "She just asks, she says."

"What?"

"Babe, when you ask, it gets done. It's your superpower."

"It's the boobs." I do my best showroom model wave at them. "Original factory equipment, turbo charged."

"It's the willingness to use them for good."

One long sniff clears my sinuses. I dab at my eyes. "You may be the best person I know, Attankat Salek. The very best."

Tan goes quiet and I again have no idea what she's thinking. I wait until I can't help myself and prod, "What?"

"Well, thinking about this scientifically," Tan begins with a pseudo-professorial tone.

"Because science matters."

"Science matters, yes, it does. And I realize that, if we decide one of us might want to give birth versus adopting, we're going to need intervention."

"Yes?"

"Well, that doesn't mean, you know, that on our own, we shouldn't still *try*."

I have to laugh. "I don't think it works that—"

She shuts me up with a kiss.

Oh, I forgot to say—I'm Lisa. Drop by the Mona Lisa next time you're in Fairbanks, and I'll personally draw you a pint. I advise summer, and you should always take my advice.

CAPTAIN OF INDUSTRY

Published: 2016
Characters: Jennifer Lamont, actress, producer, zombie killer
Suzanne Mason, tech entrepreneur
Annemarie Armgard, tech entrepreneur
Hyde Butler, actor
Setting: Hollywood and then some, California

Twenty-Seven at Last

EXTRAORDINARY THING

(February, 7 Years Later)

Every relationship has its firsts, and this was the first of all firsts. Suzanne showed her ID for a third time and waited for a receipt for her fifty bona fide United States hundred-dollar bills.

The black-eyed clerk looked as if she'd seen it all and then some, up to and including today. "You're here for *her*, aren't you?"

"Yes, ma'am." There was no need to ask who the woman meant.

As the cashier counted the bills, Suzanne counted the blessings of the situation. She was in Lancaster, sixty miles out of Hollywood, and the tabloid press was stuck in rush hour traffic she'd skipped over via helicopter.

"Wait over there." The woman pointed toward the scattering of plastic chairs as she pushed a slip of paper under the small gap at the bottom of the Plexiglas.

"Thank you."

Apparently Suzanne looked appropriately respectful because she got a glimmer of sympathy. "There's a soda machine back in the lobby. It's likely to be about twenty minutes. She'll be at the blue door."

It must have been a slow afternoon in Lancaster. The drab waiting room was empty except for her. The walls were painted that unique shade of yellow that hadn't looked clean when it first went on and showed every minute of every year since. As proof the universe was possibly on her side, the soda machine had Mountain Dew. She waited about fifteen minutes, then got two.

She'd only had a sip of hers when a buzzer sounded. A man laughed. Then she heard the sultry voice she loved answering back. When the blue door opened, the guard was covered in blushes.

Jennifer, oh Jennifer.

Her own heart still fluttered when Jennifer turned on the charm. The guard, who looked one hundred percent red-blooded dude, didn't stand a chance. The whole package was devastating. Her dark hair was still pulled up into a bundle of braids. The hem of her deep-blue gown *shooshed* against the floor as she walked. The neckline framed a sapphire-hued amulet that rested on Suzanne's favorite ever-so-shapely bosom. Add the laugh, the almost wink, the smile that failed to be demure on purpose?

My darling woman, you've still got it.

From the blue door, they went together to the Plexiglas and wire cage to claim personal belongings. Suzanne was glad to see that while they hadn't allowed Jennifer to get out of costume, they'd let her grab her handbag and day pack before bringing her here. The man who signed them out didn't look the least bit surprised when the bin also yielded up a wide belt fitted with lethal-looking gadgetry—throwing stars, daggers, and the like—that Suzanne knew had been 3D printed in heavy plastic. It was too bulky for the day pack, so Jennifer shrugged, wrapped it around her waist and smoothed up the Velcro at the back.

It did complete the outfit.

Jennifer smooched her thanks for the soda. They talked of nothing in the car that took them back to the small regional airport that had the nearest public helipad. Jennifer was busy texting and held up an exchange so Suzanne could see it.

Jennifer: *Did Lexi get home safely?*

Hyde: *Yes, she's home.*

Jennifer: *I'll call you in about 2 hours when private.*

Ninety minutes later, they landed almost two hundred miles to the south with the glistening February sun half consumed by the rolling Pacific Ocean. It was easily twenty degrees cooler than Lancaster. The onshore breeze, warm sun, and tenacious ice plant carpeting the hillsides with eye-popping violet all added up to early spring on the increasingly tropical San Diego coast.

They were home in time for dinner and a swim, even.

Apparently the press had camped out in Santa Monica, near Jennifer's condo, because there was no sign of them at the helipad in La Jolla. Another car whisked them to the ocean bluffs and the home that she and Jennifer had shared for nearly seven years.

Neither of the drivers, nor the pilot, said one word about having a fully dressed warrior-princess-elven-paladin in their vehicle. Jennifer remained uncharacteristically quiet as Suzanne rejected repeated calls from Jennifer's agent. No way was she acting as a go-between, because Jennifer wasn't yet ready to talk. She'd never made the mistake of thinking she could speak for her wife, and she wasn't starting now.

Jennifer made a beeline for the back of the house. The shower started almost immediately, and Suzanne took the time to answer the last of Annemarie's texts.

There's a perfectly reasonable explanation, she tapped out.

There always is. Annemarie had slightly warmed to Jennifer over the years. Slightly.

Like this has happened before!

Annemarie's response took just long enough for Suzanne to feel an epic eye roll through the phone. *Drama drama drama.*

Annemarie was right about one thing—life with Jennifer was not boring.

The shower stopped and she heard Jennifer's voice. Based on the worried yet unguarded tone, Suzanne guessed Jennifer was talking to Hyde Butler as promised, versus her agent or publicist. Poor Lexi Butler. She was a little kid caught in the middle of a drama she likely didn't understand.

She opened a bottle of Sonoma red, nuked a container of falafel, threw some grapes and pretzels on the plate, added a tub of pesto hummus, and carried her completed tray out to the patio table next to the pool. She was glad she'd shucked her shoes. The sun had left the terra cotta tiles the perfect temperature to keep her feet warm. After the stuffy confines of the helicopter, the air blowing in from the ocean was deeply refreshing.

A swim later would be perfect, especially since she and Jennifer were going to get an unexpected night together, due to an, uh, unscheduled, um, pause in production.

The merlot had sufficiently breathed by the time Jennifer emerged in her usual white pool wrap. She was either wearing a bikini under it or nothing at all. A hot burst of desire traveled from places south up to Suzanne's brain.

Her brain, however, had other priorities. First things first, on a day that had held the first of all firsts.

She waited until Jennifer had finished a falafel and enjoyed several swallows of wine before asking, "So why did you get arrested?"

* * *

Five Hours Earlier

"Thanks, Donna. I'll be back after lunch for afternoon makeup." Jennifer took a happy deep breath, glad to be rid of the layers of petroleum jelly and plaster to create a prosthetic mold of each ear.

The stylist was examining her handiwork with a pleased smile. "I'm sorry you had to sit through this again—thanks for being okay to do a second set. Just so you know, this afternoon I'll have to use harsher glue on your lashes, and it'll take a little longer. This morning everyone's were popping off. Ninety-two degrees in February. Thanks, climate change."

Finally out of the chair, Jennifer put her costume utility belt back on. Without it, the skirt of her long dress rode up over her backside and hips. It was not a look she had ever aspired to, even walking around a set. The discomfort of the belt was minimal, and she was already in her platform boots, maximizing comfort. The scenes where her stiletto-heeled boots would be visible were done for the day, and she appreciated being able to remain at the same height without the foot-ruining, four-inch lift.

After the necessity of being on time for your call, taking off high heels at every opportunity was a rule she'd made Lexi write down. As she'd told Suzanne last night during their evening chat, warning a six-year-old about bunions made her feel old.

"I love you in your heels," Suzanne had practically purred. "I love getting you out of them."

"That's not a lesson I'm imparting to Lexi. Hyde would kill me."

Her wife's low chuckle was a familiar balm to her soul. "Only if he got to you before Emma did."

"I'm not getting in the way of the Ultimate Mama Bear. Auntie Jen will behave," she had assured her.

She left the Featured Cast Cosmetics trailer for the short walk into the sound stage hangar. The winter sun was hot in Lancaster. It was, after all, only a couple hundred miles to Death Valley or Las Vegas, take your pick. None of the ocean breezes reached this far inland.

Inside the sound stage was another story, thankfully. The air was much cooler and the huge fans that were turned on during breaks brought welcome relief. She cut over toward catering on the left. The movie's production personal assistant who took care of Jennifer was out sick, which necessitated Jennifer picking up their own lunches. She'd grab the marked containers for both of them, and they could bask in the air-conditioning in her trailer.

She waved a general hello at today's collection of orcs and glargs. All had mastered the art of downing a sandwich and iced tea without damaging their makeup. The franchise movie was likely to do okay and get decent press. "Featured" versus "starring" money was still plenty. But she'd primarily taken the secondary role because it was being filmed near home and she was only needed on set three days out of seven.

Which had meant she and Suzanne had spent New Year's Day by the pool and enjoyed several "for no particular reason" dinner gatherings with their closest friends, including the Butlers. They'd binged *Jeopardy! Tournament of Champions* and sorted pieces for the newly opened Taj Mahal, Lego style, and finally got to catch up on *True Detective*.

No parties, no crowds, no press. Just her and the handsome, brainy love of her life.

Bliss.

When they'd had dinner at the Butlers' in Malibu, Hyde had waited until after the kids' bedtimes to ask if Auntie Jen thought working on *Valor Among Rogues* would be appropriate for six-year-old Lexi, whose interest in acting was going up in spite of all attempts to distract her for a few more years. It wouldn't take much to slide her into a pack of child elves who laugh, cry, or scream on cue.

"I think it would be perfect first exposure to what goes on behind the scenes," she'd said. "She can camp out with me. I'm sure we can work it out to match the school."

Emma still hoped that one of their kids would want to be a dentist, like her, or anything *not* a performer. It could happen with the other two, but not Lexi. Lexi was Hyde Butler's kid all the way to the core. She had a terrific memory, a natural sense of performance, and her father's way with both a smile and a laser-eye.

"We really need you to show her that the acting life is not all red-carpet walks and Instagram selfies," Emma had pleaded.

"I promise—there will be no sugar-coating reality."

"You really do have to get up at five a.m.," Jennifer had therefore told Lexi when the alarm went off Monday morning in the suite they shared at the nearest hotel that had one. "By the time we get to the set, you'll see that dozens of people have already been working for an hour. It's mean to them if we're late, and it costs a lot of money. You don't have to fake play nice, but you *must* be professional."

Be on time, don't be mean, and don't get bunions. Three important lessons Jennifer wished someone had told her back in her modeling days. To Lexi's credit, she'd not complained one word this morning, the third day in a row with the early wake-up. Rather, she'd been glum that it was her last day.

On the catering table Jennifer's smoked salmon salad was labeled and under the watchful eye of one of the staff. So far she had no complaints about the care the production company took with the cast and crew. A production this size was a lot like a small town, and everyone had to do their bit to keep everyone safe as the train of filming barreled down the track.

Lexi's lunch was still there as well. Half mac and cheese, half broccoli. She picked it up and looked around.

The young man in the crisp blue bow tie, who was likely hoping to break into acting via catering, noticed her glance. He no doubt knew exactly whose kid Lexi was. He seemed to notice everything, which was good when there was food you didn't want anyone messing with before it got to its intended recipient. He cleared his throat before volunteering, "She was about to get it when Dane Pruitt brought her some pink sheets and they went somewhere to go over them."

"When was this?"

"A couple of minutes ago, maybe?"

Pink sheets? First she'd heard of another round of script revisions. Perhaps her set was in her trailer. Why would an assistant director be bringing them? Because his own PA was out sick like hers? But the script supervisor wouldn't have handed them off to an AD like Pruitt, who'd been around the biz for probably two decades. Not to mention that any AD with half an ego would not have agreed to deliver script changes, and she'd yet to meet any director who didn't have an abundant supply of ego.

On the other hand, Pruitt did have an excessive "nice guy, here to help" vibe, which fit his attempt to dress a decade younger than he was. Who in Hollywood didn't? Still, delivering script changes? There must have been a good reason.

She took their lunches back to her trailer, but no pink sheets were waiting for her. Lexi's scenes were all with the elven group. If one person had changes, all of them got the changes. Confused, she navigated her way out of the rows of cast trailers and past the production offices housed in double-wide temporary buildings. She was all the way back inside the sound stage hangar when she spotted the script supervisor.

"I didn't get my pink sheets."

Hina looked confused. "That's because there aren't any?"

She cocked her head. "Lexi was given some and I can't find her now."

"Says who?"

She glanced toward the catering area. Had the young man in the bow tie gotten it wrong? It was a weirdly specific thing to misremember. "I was told Dane Pruitt had them for her."

Hina blinked her eyes in surprise as she began to shake her head no. Her lips pressed into a hard line.

Panic sent fire down her spine. "What?"

"You should find her."

"What do you know?" Her heart was pounding an alarm so high in her ears she could hardly hear.

"What do I know? That he and one of the producers were at UCLA together, and he's got some hard-luck story about being misunderstood and out of work because he was unjustly canceled."

"Canceled? Over what?"

Hina grimaced. "How he mentors younger cast members."

Move, Jen, move.

She only barely heard Hina saying, "I'll try to find him."

The sensation of being frozen snapped. Gasping with dread and shock, Jennifer bolted across the sound stage to the catering area.

"Are you absolutely certain you saw Assistant Director Dane Pruitt with pink sheets for Lexi?"

"Oh, yes," he said immediately. "I hadn't seen changes get all the way to pink yet, so that was a thing."

She was already backing away. Already choking on horrific thoughts. Mentoring younger cast members—was that what it was called now to avoid words like "grooming" and worse? She sucked in as deep a breath as she could manage and put the entire power of her diaphragm behind her shout. "Lexi Butler, where are you?"

All the heads turned, of course they did. She was never *not* aware of people watching her, that was her life, and in this case she *meant* them to look and wanted them to be alarmed about Lexi's absence. She ran as fast as she could toward the exit to the trailers, calling Lexi's name.

Of all the things Hyde and Emma had worried about, the one they hadn't mentioned, but Jennifer nevertheless understood, was her seeing or experiencing anything that ruined her innocent trust in people. Was it possible to protect innocence without naming the most insidious harm?

Her feet were still sluggish. Her arms swung like lead. There was a contract item that forbade anyone on production premises being alone with cast or crew under the age of 18. She'd had to get a waiver to be alone with Lexi in her trailer. Hyde and Emma had signed off on it. What would an assistant director have to discuss with a child performer?

Nothing, that's what.

She pounded up the stairs into the production office. The gaggle of assistants regarded her in surprise. "Is Lexi Butler here?"

The director came out of his office, a sandwich in one hand.

"Where's Dane Pruitt? He took Lexi somewhere to discuss pink sheets that don't exist! Where is he? Where is Lexi?"

"He did what now?"

Jennifer was already out the door. She didn't know which way Pruitt's trailer was.

Ian, the security guard who patrolled the trailer area, tried to get in her way. "Can I help, Ms. Lamont?"

"Where's Pruitt's trailer?"

"Third down on Row B—wait up!"

She rounded the corner to Row B at the fastest run she could manage in full-length skirts and platform boots. She'd had lots of practice but still felt as if she were slogging through mud.

The door on Trailer Three was closed and the blinds were tightly shut.

She threw herself at the door and yanked the knob. It was locked.

"Lexi! Lexi, are you in there?" She used both fists to pound on it.

A moment later the door opened, and Pruitt leaned out, the expression on his bloodless face one of perfect amazement and innocence. "What's going on?"

"Is Lexi Butler in there?"

"Uh, why—"

It was a yes or no question and he was taking too long. She seized the front of his polo shirt and yanked him down the steps of the trailer as she propelled herself up and past him.

The air-conditioning wasn't on—it was stifling hot. Lexi, her mouth open and eyes very wide, had naturally taken off the light long-sleeve sun shirt she wore over her close-fitting elf costume. There was a glass of ice and an open can of sparkling watermelon water.

"Aunt Jen?"

"No closed doors. No food or drink not from catering or me." She bent over, hands on her thighs, catching her breath. "This isn't your fault, Lexi, sweetie. You're not in trouble. But those are the rules your parents emphasized, remember?"

"He said the AC was broken, and I said he should open the door, but all he did was close the blinds, and he gave me the water after saying he was sorry he'd got a text that the pink sheets were pulled back, and I'd walked all this way."

Jennifer was relieved to hear unease in Lexi's recounting. The little girl had sensed something wasn't right and damn it that she had to even worry. The trailers were all the same and Jennifer flipped the switch to turn on the portable air-conditioning unit. It promptly whirred into life.

"Honey, this isn't your fault, okay? I'm angry at that guy, not you. He broke the rules, and it's his job to know he shouldn't."

The old boys' network had let that creep onto the set. The producer friend who'd arranged it probably wasn't even here to see what they'd set into motion.

She was so angry her fingertips trembled. Her head felt as if there was no blood in it. That creep was lucky none of the stage weapons on her belt was real.

There was the wrath of Jennifer, but it was *nothing* compared to the wrath of Emma Butler and the power of Hyde Butler, the man with half a billion in box office last year.

She ought to have said, "Stay here," but she didn't.

Pruitt was proclaiming to the security guard his bewilderment at Jennifer's rough treatment of him. "It's a hot day and the kid looked parched. What's the harm?"

"You locked the door," Jennifer hissed as other cast and crew arrived, forming a semicircle around the trailer door. "You took a minor into your trailer, which is a contract violation. It's a *union* violation, and she's protected under all the child actor clauses I'm sure you know by heart. You locked the door. You lied to her about the broken AC and got your jollies from her taking her sun shirt off."

"You're sick in the head if you imagine that kind of thing! That door's been locking all by itself since I got here. What's your problem?"

"You were overheard telling her there were pink sheets to go over. There are no pink sheets and there never were."

"Whoever said that is making it up. They must have a grudge against me." He shrugged an appeal to the growing crowd of onlookers.

"Catering staff heard you."

"These cancel culture types! You can't be a white straight guy in this business anymore. Lying, crazy bitch—"

* * *

"And that's when I punched him," Jennifer finished. "I don't regret it, but Lexi saw me, and it scared the crap out of her. Real violence, and Auntie Jen doing it."

Suzanne lifted Jennifer's left hand to survey the red knuckles. "You didn't even break the skin. Otherwise I'd insist you get a rabies shot from contact with that guy."

Jennifer made that sound that said she understood Suzanne was trying to distract her a little with humor. "He's a jackal. Though that's probably an insult to jackals to say so."

"Someone called the cops?"

"He insisted. They showed up, and I said, 'Yes, I hit him,' and here we are."

Suzanne felt Jennifer sigh. Her libido wanted this conversation to pause for the rest of the evening. The night air was cooling, and Jennifer's body was warm and supple as they shared the chaise. She wanted to escape from her own rage at what had happened.

Instead she reached for the wine, knowing they'd both get sleepy. But it meant that later they'd probably wake, and all the wonder and glory of Jennifer in her arms was very likely to happen then. "You're all over the web now."

"Is his name attached?"

"Yes."

"Good. My agent has booked me on *LA Today* in the morning. I will be speaking only the facts. Happy to pay a fine. Happy to do time, and I'll simply keep repeating the facts until he's out of the business forever, and the sight of his face instills unease in anyone unfortunate enough to see it."

"Unless…" Suzanne was familiar with the diplomacy it took to move Jennifer off a decided course of action. "Have you thought about Lexi? No doubt she's already traumatized and blaming herself."

"This is—oh." Jennifer muttered an expletive. "It was her last day, and she got sent home before her final scene. Someone else got her two lines." After a long pause she added quietly, "Well, hell. She's got to be thinking she's the one getting punished."

Suzanne topped up Jennifer's wine.

She savored a sip. "How do we do this? Needing to protect the child's privacy is how these guys get away with their ick. They make the kids feel safe and understood when they're six, see them again on another set, and wait for the right time to 'keep a secret.' They *count* on silence. Apparently, he's got rumors, but all he has to do is say it's a lie, find a buddy to pity him, and there's nobody who wants to name and shame. And I so very much want to shame."

"What about the production putting out a blanket statement saying they've separated him from production for violation of contract?"

"He'll claim it's a witch hunt and move on to another set and another kid."

"What did Emma say? Or did you talk to Hyde?"

"Both at the same time. They're livid and scared. They didn't say so, but the reality is that even with Auntie Jen looking out for her, Lexi wasn't safe. I was getting molded for a future makeup job, so the creep knew I didn't have eyes on her. Maybe all he was after was proving control—he could get her to take her overshirt off. But what if?"

The horror in Jennifer's voice was a match to what Suzanne felt. "What might have happened is unthinkable. Oh, honey." With that Suzanne realized Jennifer was crying. She used her sleeve to dab gently at a stray tear and earned a damp smooch.

"It might have happened when I was supposed to be her protector. How would I live with myself? Emma and Hyde would never forgive themselves either. And these creeps. *These creeps.* Most of the time getting away with theft of the most precious of things."

The tears didn't last long, and Suzanne was aware that under the dark hair at her shoulder Jennifer's brain was firing on all cylinders. A new plan would be drawn up, and all Jennifer's being would be set to see it through.

Finally, Jennifer sat up. After another bite of hummus-dredged falafel, she said, "I'll call Emma again about what I think we should do, starting with a clear message that any press that tries to talk to Lexi will never talk to or photograph Hyde

Butler again. All the coverage should be adults talking about what adults aren't supposed to do. Let's keep her name out of it if we can, and make sure *his* name is all over it."

* * *

From the wings of the studio, Suzanne watched the morning show co-host, perched in a director's chair, give Jennifer a serious look. "What do you say to people who think that violence was the wrong way to handle the situation?"

Jennifer was likewise perched, her long legs crossed and showing off Suzanne's favorite ankle boots. "I agree. I'd been terrified, and then he lied to my face about his actions and accused me of being unreasonable in my fear. Oh yes, and that I was out to get him on a witch hunt. I lost my head, and I punched him in the nose. I shouldn't have."

"Would you do it again?"

"I'd rather never have to worry about a kid in our profession again. Our silence is their power, so I'm being loud about how unacceptable Dane Pruitt's behavior was."

"Some people online are calling you a hero."

Jennifer made a face. "I'm not. I protected a kid and that's the very least a decent human being should do. It's not heroic—it's what we owe each other, at a minimum."

The interviewer inclined her head as if she agreed. "Do you think this will affect the movie release?"

"Not at all. I have another two weeks before I'm done, and it's going to wrap on schedule end of next month. Like the first movie, it's a fun romp with trickery and epic fails, a little romance, and great stunts."

"Did you do your own stunts?"

"The easy ones, sure. But I'm not an idiot. I leave the tricky ones to the pros!"

In Suzanne's opinion, given Jennifer's commitment to training over many years, the creep was lucky he'd only gotten a bloody nose. He didn't even have a black eye, and charges against

Jennifer had been dropped when he'd failed to follow through on filing a complaint. For her part, she'd happily amplified #OnceAgainNotaDragQueen online. The usual asshats were saying "Not all men" and complaining it was nothing more than a witch hunt against a guy without anything ever going to court.

Those people weren't getting a lot of traction, not when the guy had sealed his social media fate when he'd ranted about "these women" into someone's phone as he shoved a tissue up his bloody nose. It was a hunt, to be sure, and it was the witches, the furies, the bitches, and brats who were not going to lose his scent. *Into the trebuchet with you, my dude.*

The studio went to commercial break, and Jennifer shook hands with her interviewer as they parted ways.

"That went well," Suzanne observed.

"Yes, it did." Jennifer cocked her head. "You were staring at the boots."

"Yes, I was."

"She had on some sweet Choos."

"I didn't notice."

She got the full-on, wide, eyes aglow smile then. "What are you thinking now?"

"That you are an extraordinary thing and I'm still falling." Brave and fierce, she wanted to add, but her throat tightened.

Jennifer rewarded her with a smooch. "To tell you the truth, I can't wait to get the boots off."

"I do enjoy that too. Have you forgotten what day it is?"

"Right now I couldn't tell you what *month* it is."

Before Suzanne could tell her, Jennifer blinked and added, "It's Valentine's Day. You had a special date all planned."

"We can cancel. There will be some lucky couple on the wait list."

"We can still go out."

"And have press sidling up to the table the whole time? No thank you."

They slid out the studio doors just before the ad break ended. It felt as if they were alone in a corridor full of bustling people.

Jennifer looked up through her lashes. "Since I ruined your plans, I think it's up to me to plan the evening."

Suzanne smiled down into her favorite pair of eyes. "What do you want to do?"

"It starts with getting out of these boots and, um, other inconvenient articles of clothing." A suggestively soft sound not quite a purr was followed by, "What do *you* want?"

Those eyes.

A long, languid, melting caress of those expressive, dark eyes, bronze and gold swirling in their depths, traveled over Suzanne's mouth, to her shoulders, to her hips. A softly indrawn breath and parting of the lush red lips sent a tingling shock wave over her skin, the same way they had from the first moment she'd held Jennifer in her arms.

Truth, then. "I want to spend the day making you dissolve."

Those eyes and that knowing laugh.

"Not if I melt you first."

SIMPLY THE BEST

Published:	2021
Characters:	Pepper Addington (Paddington), intern, executive assistant
	Alice Paul Cabot, science journalist
	Barbara Paul Cabot, journalist and Alice's mother
	Helene Jolie, Founder and CEO, Simply the Best
Setting:	Los Angeles, California, and New York City, New York

Thirty is a new beginning.

ALL THAT AND A MILKSHAKE

(March, 4 Years Later)

"I don't think we're getting in today."

"Neither do I." Pepper gazed up at the very tall, very solid, and very locked gate. It had to be twenty feet to the top, and that was before a person would reach the additional four feet of barbed wire.

"It occurs to me…"

Alice's tone was nonchalant, but Pepper wasn't fooled. "Yes?"

"Juana is a paper calendar kind of gal. I was happy she even responded to an email. For someone who's listening to the sounds of the universe, she's surprisingly averse to tech. So it's possible that we didn't make it to her datebook. And I should have confirmed with her last night, but I got distracted."

"By what?"

"You."

That was fair. "I have no regrets. But now it's looking like that phone call might have been necessary. Event planning is all in the follow-through." Pepper gazed to her left and right at the fencing that ran without a break in both directions until curving out of sight. Their sturdy Jeep was the only source of shade, aside from the lanky-armed saguaros and knee-high thorn bushes on the other side of the narrow, dusty New Mexico road.

She pointed at the speaker mounted on the left-hand gate post. "Should we maybe wake up that keypad and see if someone answers?"

"Trust me, someone already knows we're here. Smile for the camera. Cameras."

As Alice pointed them out, Pepper saw that in addition to the obvious camera above the keypad there were at least six more pointed at the gate area. The sharp desert sun no doubt illuminated them both very clearly. "Do you think we've already been scanned, facially recognized, and pings sent to, like, CIA, MI6, and so forth?"

"Yup."

A gust of dry, warm wind threatened to pull her floppy sun hat off her head. Pepper tugged it back into place. Alice's hats stayed on her head. How Alice managed that was a mystery to Pepper. As they'd traveled the width and height of the Americas over the last four years, Alice's ability to remain prepared and tidy, even in the foulest of weather, had left Pepper deeply impressed. It never failed to make her want to muss Alice's hair or unbutton something.

What was it about khaki shorts with a million pockets and a seersucker Madras plaid button-up that was so dead sexy?

Alice turned her back to the gate and surveyed the landscape. "It rained a couple of days ago. See the desert marigold under that bunch of mesquite?"

Pepper followed the line of Alice's finger to see the bright spots of yellow just above the dry ground. "It's so hopeful. Waiting for rain, and content to exist without asking anything of, well, anything." During their first long sojourn when Pepper had been between jobs, Pepper had learned that a seemingly barren landscape showed all its life if you stood still.

Alice, she'd also learned, was very good at standing still. She noticed everything and perpetually asked all the journalism questions: How, who, what, where, why, when—and back to how. Always *how*. Rocks, atoms, electronics, high-speed light pulses, stars, planets—Alice was curious about all of it. Given that her father had been a scientist and her mother was still an active journalist and biographer, it wasn't really a surprise.

Fortunately, Pepper knew, Alice brought that same curiosity and wonder to life with Pepper. Last night, in their high desert motel, instead of confirming their appointment today, Alice had likely been asking, "Which feels better? Here? Or there?"

Between gasps, Pepper had answered, "Here—a little. There—a lot."

"So a little bit of this and a lot of that?"

Her legs limp and hands clutching the surprisingly sturdy motel bed headboard, she'd felt like the ceiling fan revolving over their heads. She was spinning in complete harmony and safety around the center point of Alice's fingers.

How...where... *Oh, right there.*

Grateful for the evaporating effect of the desert wind on the back of her neck, Pepper treated herself to a playback of the pleasure of Alice's meticulous attentions. She remembered the first time she'd seen Alice, looking very out of place, rumpled, and undoubtedly annoyed. As a masculine-of-center woman and a science journalist, her normal habitat didn't include places like the Simply the Best corporate complex. The lush, sculpted California campus was devoted to all things hyper-feminine—for those who could afford it, of course. Pepper still couldn't believe she'd spent a year of her life in that almost make-believe environment, working for celebrity founder Helene Jolie.

She'd thought she'd been living her perfect life.

She'd been right, and then she'd been wrong. Alice, along with her adorable, abundant geekery, had been nothing but right for her ever since.

Next week they both had to go back to reality. Pepper had two clients with upcoming events. Alice had been commissioned by a journal to do a series on new frontiers for science, so she was going to Hamburg to spend a week with condensed matter researchers.

"It's not like I haven't seen the Very Large Array before," Alice was saying. "It's not actually that much to *see*. Except that it is. I think you'd get it."

"Even if I don't, I get that *you're* awed and inspired. It did look really interesting in *Contact*." She grinned as she recalled watching the movie for the first time as a companion to planning the itinerary for this trip. Alice had eagerly explained what Carl Sagan had gotten right more than thirty years earlier, what the movie screwed up, and fast forwarded through any scene that didn't have Jodie Foster in it, as well as all scenes where Jodie Foster was making out with a guy.

Alice abruptly cocked her head, and then Pepper heard the whine of an approaching vehicle from beyond the gate.

"You were right. A welcome party is on the way. Maybe Juana is part of it?"

"She's not answering her phone, so it could be possible. But I'm doubtful."

"Maybe you shouldn't have been pointing at the cameras like you were casing the joint."

Alice *hmm*ed as she reapplied lip balm, prompting Pepper to do the same thing. The wind was sapping every bit of moisture out of her skin. After only ten minutes or so, the sun was making her wish she'd applied a heavier layer of sunscreen on the exposed parts of her pale arms. The moment she'd turned thirty, her easy-to-tan skin had turned into easy-to-burn. She envied the even, light brown of Alice's skin, and she loved how kissable it was too.

"I'll grant you, in retrospect, that pointing out the cameras might not have been wise."

"I'm holding you to your promise of legit enchiladas Christmas-style tonight. I mean *legit*."

"The green sauce is going to make you cry."

"Spicy green sauce is why the universe sent us sour cream." Pepper did her very best to look unarmed and nonthreatening. "My insistence, though, is not so much about the enchiladas as it is about how much I would like *not* to be in a holding cell."

"That's extremely unlikely. Nevertheless, I understand."

The sound of the unseen vehicle was getting louder. Pepper wasn't truly worried. Of course the VLA had tight security, and its international ties gave a wide spectrum of interests a reason to keep it secure. Pepper wouldn't be surprised to learn that their Jeep had been noted the moment they'd left the highway a few miles back. The cracked paved road ended at these gates. Alice had said that the first of the deep space radar dishes was another six miles beyond.

The vehicle clanked to a stop on the other side of the solid gate. After a moment the gate swung inward a few feet and stopped. The only occupant of the dusty Humvee was a stocky, barrel-chested man in camo fatigues who waited a moment before getting out of the vehicle. He sized them up and nodded a greeting. There was a no-nonsense pistol holstered on his hip. "Do you have business here today?"

"I thought I did," Alice answered. "An appointment with Doctor Juana Altepeh. But maybe she forgot?"

"What is the purpose of your visit?"

"An insider tour and an interview on where the VLA is right now. I'm Alice Cabot. I'm a journalist. I've visited before, but my companion hasn't."

At the gesture her way Pepper said, "Pepper Addington, science fan."

"You must be, because this is a long way from anywhere." He surveyed them, then reluctantly shook his head. "I don't have the clearance to take you in, and Dr. Altepeh isn't here. Her mother had a medical issue, and she's home in Cuernavaca."

Alice's expression was both annoyed and compassionate all at once. "Of course I understand. She'll owe me."

With a glance at the landscape that reinforced how far it was from anywhere, the guard said, "You maybe should have confirmed with her?"

Alice nodded, her face absent of any hint of why she hadn't, which Pepper appreciated. "Yes, that would have been prudent."

"You need water? I have some bottles in a cooler."

"So do we," Pepper said. "Thanks for the offer."

As the guard began to turn away, Alice asked, "The diner in Magdalena just off the highway is still open, right?"

His eyes narrowed as he took stock of the two of them again. "It would be, if it wasn't Monday."

Pepper put her hands on her hips and scowled at Alice. "Now you're in trouble. Promises were made."

The guard chuckled politely. "Try Carlita's in Socorio. Sopaipillas the size of a cantaloupe."

Pepper nodded approvingly. "This nice man has saved you from going on probation."

He gave them a cheery wave and the gate swung closed.

"He didn't even ask to see our credentials."

"I don't think he needed to."

Pepper reached for Alice's hand and loved how easily their fingers laced together. "We have a whole day with no plans."

"Except enchiladas."

"There is that." Pepper squeezed her hand before letting go. "Other thoughts?"

"How about a movie?"

Alice appeared to consider it seriously. "You mean inside, out of the sun? Sitting down in the dark?"

"Yeah, like that."

"Great idea."

Pepper pulled Alice to her for a kiss. After their lips parted, she murmured, "I thought, why not give them something to talk about?"

* * *

Carlita's was everything down-home New Mexico could be. The small restaurant was right off the dust-swirling highway. The inside was whitewashed walls, sealed concrete floors, and tables painted red, green, or white. The aroma of roasting peppers and spices mingled with fruit and baking bread, setting off hunger spasms in Alice's stomach.

Their orders of enchiladas Christmas-style arrived in no time, served on thick paper plates and topped with scoops of sour cream and guacamole. Pepper was already making delighted yum-yum noises over the brick-red sauce that smothered the beef and cheddar. Alice started on the chicken and jack covered in bright, limey, spicy green sauce.

"Everything you hoped for?"

"Yes. So good," Pepper answered between bites. Just then a platter of sopaipillas, with honey and butter on the side, went past the table.

Alice laughed as Pepper's gaze followed the dish all the way to its destination.

"Ours are ordered."

Pepper dabbed sour cream off her upper lip. "You do get points that you were absolutely right. A roadside diner anywhere in New Mexico has better enchiladas than the swanky cafeteria at Simply the Best."

Alice dipped her head in thanks, always glad to earn points with Pepper. She'd lost a few yesterday. A long hike to see petroglyphs on a remote trail near Three Rivers had proved the guidebook guilty of overstating the quantity and visibility of the most distant collections. Even though the main site was glorious with thousands of them, they'd both been footsore by then.

Alice was aware that Pepper wasn't really keeping any kind of score, but she wouldn't blame Pepper if she did, given the mistakes Alice had made when they first met. There'd been words said that couldn't be taken back, even after they were forgiven. It didn't change things that some of those words—particularly about Pepper's boss, Helene Jolie—had been right.

The voice of her mother popped into her head to ask, "Maybe you're the one who's keeping score in this relationship?"

As with all visitations of her mother's undoubted wisdom, Alice already knew the answer—the feeling of having to continually earn Pepper's approval was her problem—and not of Pepper's making. Pepper was an open book, a trait Alice dearly and deeply loved. If she said the entire day had been fun, exhausting, and that maybe she didn't need to see more petroglyphs for a while, Alice could trust that Pepper wasn't holding her accountable for the blister that had popped up on Pepper's heel.

Also true—constantly telling herself she needed to stay on Pepper's good side suggested that a bad side existed. Could Pepper be cranky when hungry, snappish before coffee, and outright peevish if someone not her took the last of the marmalade? Yes, but it wasn't in her nature to be cruel or vicious. She didn't hold onto grudges to deliver payback later.

"Hey." Pepper nudged the back of Alice's hand with a fingertip. "Where'd you go?"

"Thinking. And wallowing in how rich this red sauce is."

"Is there a movie—" Pepper paused as the server stopped at the table.

He topped up her water glass. "Your sopaipillas will be up in a couple of minutes. Did you want anything else?"

Alice hurriedly swallowed the tortilla chip she'd dunked in green sauce. "If you were going to see a movie that's out, where would you go near here?"

The wiry young man gave it some thought as he filled Alice's water glass. "The multiplex down the highway is closest. But I wouldn't say 'near.' Nothing's near to here. Ya gotta keep the gas tank full."

Pepper nodded. "This is true."

"My *tía abuela* owns the museum next door. You don't need any gas to get there." He dug in his pocket and pulled out a handful of yellow coupons. "You get a free homemade milkshake from the snack bar if you pay admission."

Pepper accepted the slip of paper. "Free milkshake, you say?"

"Made from ice cream and milk in a blender with vanilla a *prima* sends up from Paplantla."

"Thanks!" As the young man moved to the next table, Pepper turned her bright brown gaze on Alice and wiggled her eyebrows. "A museum. *And* a milkshake."

"What's not to like? It's out of the sun. We learn something. We consume even more good food. Let's."

"Before you commit…" She pushed the coupon across the table.

Alice glanced and thought, well, it would make Pepper very happy. "The Museum of Lipstick?"

"Aren't you curious?"

"About lipstick?" Alice had only given lipstick a thought in one context. "If it's on you, very much so, because it ends up on my lips sooner or later. Often sooner. Which, to be very clear, I do enjoy."

She got a slow, amused blink in response.

* * *

The museum was housed in a squat, square building that Pepper had taken for a mini-mart. The structure had a slight tilt to it, as if it had yielded over time to the prevailing desert wind. The paint was sand-chipped and sun-faded, but the windows were spotless. A cheerful bell sounded as she opened the front door. Instead of a ticket booth there was a snack bar with a handwritten menu tacked to the wall behind it.

An elderly woman with sharp black eyes turned on a stool to face them. She tucked a bookmark into her hardback and smiled a greeting. "*Buenas dias.* How may I help you?"

"We have a coupon." Pepper handed it over. "Your great-nephew persuaded us to visit."

"He's a good boy, that one. I bet he didn't tell you he makes the sopaipilla dough every day."

"He didn't say a word, and they were delicious." Pepper happily paid the admission fee, all the while admiring the woman's thick silver and black braids which set off long earrings of turquoise stones wrapped in a white-beaded silver wire. They'd look nowhere near as good against her own increasingly thin and not so blond hair. All the product in the world wasn't going to change the genes she'd inherited from her mother.

"The exhibit is most interesting if you travel it clockwise. Enjoy!"

Alice held the door to let Pepper precede her into the main room. Jeweler display cases lined three walls, interspersed with vintage advertising posters on easels. They had the place to themselves.

"'Founded in 2004 with a small-business grant and donations from local and national brands to augment a private collection,'" Pepper read aloud from the information placard alongside the first display. She bent slightly to look at preparations of balms and tints made with the likely ingredients and processes as those found in Egyptian tombs.

"I'd expect a museum like this in Manhattan," Alice observed.

"There might well be. There's a cosmetics exhibit at the Smithsonian, I think. I remember sending correspondence for Helene to a curator."

Alice pointed at the list of ingredients. "Lead. Malachite. Both toxic, especially over time."

"Worn by men and women," Pepper added.

Pepper was aware that Alice's entire beauty regimen consisted of castor oil shampoo, beeswax lip balm, and moisturizing SPF 50 sunscreen. Intense study of cosmetics wasn't Alice's general cup of tea. She also knew that Alice wouldn't hurry her because she was bored by it. At any given moment Alice could open some well of scientific debate she was carrying around in her brain and sift through it to amuse herself while Pepper enjoyed the museum.

She paused in front of a full-size standing cutout from the 1950s proclaiming, "Max Factor Makes the Difference!" The model was a bombshell blonde, complete with a bullet bra. Vibrant red lips, carefully penciled eyebrow arches, and demure touches of rouge were accompanied by a gorgeous Italian haircut, cat's eye sunglasses, and clinging pedal pushers. "Oo-la-la."

"There's no subtlety in the cosmetics-equals-sex appeal, is there?"

"Not back then and not now. Do you think I'd look good in that haircut?"

"Is this a trick question?"

She glanced at Alice. "Why do you ask?"

Alice had an endearing habit of looking left when she made one point, then right when she made the next, as if going back and forth between lists of pros and cons. "Because it's true that I think you look desirable in whatever you choose to wear or however you do your hair. I also know that saying 'you look good in everything' is not a winning answer. Nor is it exactly a compliment for me to say I'd never get bored if you walked around in that black slip of yours every day, all day."

"Are you trying to take my breath away?" That black slip was a guaranteed fire starter. She risked another look and met a smoldering glance that said Alice was recalling any number of times that Alice had driven her into a frenzy by telling Pepper to leave it on until Alice gave her permission to remove it.

"Yes, of course."

She managed a shaky breath and whispered, "Stop that."

"Why?"

"So you want me to be thinking about that for the rest of the afternoon?"

"I absolutely do."

They were alone, but making out, or attempting anything adventurous in whatever bathroom might be available, wasn't going to be sufficient. Besides, though she might protest waiting, yearning was its own reward when she knew that Alice would make it worth her while. "As long as you are thinking about it too."

At that Alice let out a chagrined laugh, breaking the spell of desire she wove so easily. "I'll be honest. My imagination is hampered by the fact that my stomach is full, I need a Tums, and there's a milkshake in my future as well. So it's going to be a while before anything is fast or furious."

"Let's find somewhere to have a walk in a while. A nice, gentle walk."

"Good idea, that is, if your blister is doing okay."

"I'm good and thank you for the kind ministrations last night."

"I suppose *ministrations* is one way to put it."

Two cases further on, Pepper was delighted to find a display of recent lipstick compacts and tubes that included several from Simply the Best's past ten years. She snapped a couple of pictures. "I'll send it to Helene because I think this would please her. Their new line of reusable containers is such a good idea. It's a throwback good for sustainability. Even dime store compacts had replaceable palettes back in the olden days. Not that these are dime store." She waved a hand at the display. "Those are real opal chips inset in the covers."

Alice made a noncommittal noise. Pepper wasn't sure if it was because she was dubious about the claim of sustainability on the lipstick's accompanying box or because Helene Jolie was probably Alice's least favorite person.

She supposed it was not important to know which it was. It was probably both. From Pepper's perspective, since she had left Simply the Best Helene had lived up to the terms of Pepper's separation from the company, including acting as a reference for clients Pepper was wooing for her event consulting career. She didn't play that card often, but every time she had, the contract had been promptly signed, with commensurate high expectations and high remuneration from the client.

At the final display case they found a personal collection of cosmetic containers that had been handed down over five generations from mothers to daughters. The showpiece was an opulent lipstick compact with a matching horse-hair application brush.

Pepper pressed a hand to her heart as she read aloud, "'This sterling silver- and gold-embellished compact for lip rouge, and the matching brush, were carved by my grandmother's father from turquoise given to him and my great-grandmother as a wedding gift in 1903. My daughter said it was so precious it ought to be in a museum. So I made a museum for it.' I think that's the sweetest family story I've ever heard about an heirloom."

"How many times must it have been touched and enjoyed over the decades after being made by an artisan in the family,"

Alice mused. "Leave it to you to find such a simple experience and make it…"

"What?"

"All that *and* a milkshake."

* * *

Alice was happy to rejoin the museum owner at the snack bar. She needed to sit down for a bit. Something was forming in her brain—a hypothesis had been circling the past few days and wanted to find words. Her brain tended to churn through data to seek out revelations, which felt simultaneously frightening and welcome.

The owner flashed them a pleased smile as she dropped another scoop of ice cream into an already half-full blender. "Did you enjoy it?"

"Very much," Pepper assured her. "I hope it's okay that I took pictures of the Simply the Best display. I used to work for the CEO, and I think she'd be charmed. She does try to ensure that every aspect of a product has pleasing features."

As always, when Jolie's name was mentioned people wanted to know more about her, and the museum's owner was no exception. Alice would never not think of that woman as a straight-up villain, but fairness insisted that she accept Jolie was addressing the issues that Alice had challenged her about. Including a firm corporate policy about fairness to interns. They were now paid more than a quarterly stipend and not allowed to be used in roles permanent benefit-earning staff ought to hold—well, Alice had been right about all of it. The cost of the change hadn't even blipped the earnings, and a lot of Los Angeles community college and state university students were now able to afford career-making internships that had formerly gone to private and prestige school alums who could live without a paycheck.

But what was bubbling her brain wasn't about Jolie or the past. She thought several times to try to explain it to Pepper because that seemed to be the only way she'd make sense of it. Every time she thought to try, however, her gut told her to stop because Pepper was at the center of the confusion.

"What were you thinking about?" Pepper slurped at the last of her milkshake as she settled into the rental car driver seat. "Lipstick, toxic chemicals, and the rise and fall of civilizations that used them?"

Alice turned her head away, surprised by the sting of tears.

"Hey." Pepper put the key in the ignition but didn't turn it. "What's wrong?"

"Nothing. I promise. I think…"

Bless her, Pepper didn't push. It was such a gift she had, for reading people and situations.

"I think…" *Don't censor. Say the words that want to come out.* "This is going to work."

"I'm not sure what 'this' means. Like, if we go for a walk and have a shower, we can get out my black slip—that will work?"

Alice choked on a laugh. "I know *that* will work." *Don't be a coward.*

Pepper started the car and turned on the air-conditioning but made no attempt to put it in gear.

The cool air helped the ache behind Alice's eyes. She finally found the courage to face this woman, the one she had known would always see through her. "By *this* I mean *us*."

Pepper shook her head slightly. Alice realized then that Pepper had never doubted, not from the moment they'd finally gotten their wires uncrossed. For her, the past was where it belonged, all the way behind them. She had no context for the revelation Alice was finally accepting. "What are you trying to say?"

"I just—it's been—I knew we would be so good for each other. I *know* that I love you and you love me. So I'm wondering why today, for some reason, I finally feel as if I accept it."

"Oh." There was only patience and thoughtfulness in Pepper's eyes.

"Today was completely upended and every minute was still great. I was thinking, well, it's always great with you. And then

I asked myself why I thought I wasn't part of the reason why it was great. That I thought it was *you* making everything so terrific, not *us*." She ended out of breath and feeling an absolute fool for talking about something that, said aloud, seemed like simple semantics. Except that it wasn't.

Pepper's lips twitched, but there was not one shred of mockery. "Now I get it."

"Get what?"

"Something your mother said when we met."

"I can imagine a lot of things she might have said."

"She didn't say much, but what she did say, well—"

"It wasn't frivolous, I'm sure."

"She said that you were the only person she knew that could argue so hard against love. That I should trust her when she said she'd never seen you *in* love before. And she was looking at me with that look, you know, with the owl-eye glasses, and like I'm the focus of her entire being at that moment."

Alice knew the look. "She wasn't wrong." Finally, clarity began to sort out data and emotions. What had been a thousand tiny red dots became clean blue lines connecting history, experience, life, cause, and effect. *You dummy*, she chided herself. *Of course talking to Pepper helps.* "I've been telling myself I didn't deserve you, so how could I deserve *us*."

Pepper dropped her hands into her lap. "Wow."

They were silent for a few moments. Alice closed her eyes. The tight, hard feeling in her chest eased as she pictured a gentle tide washing over a parched, baked shore and filling in the cracks with cool, healing life.

Pepper broke the silence. "And do you now think you deserve us? What we have?"

"Not entirely." She laughed with chagrin. "Give me a couple of minutes."

"I'll even give you the rest of the day. Or, how about the rest of my life?"

Alice snapped open her eyes. Pepper was gazing at her with a vulnerable tenderness. "Are you..?"

Pepper raised her eyebrows. "I am suggesting we plan on this working forever."

"Yes."

"Yes to what?"

"I hope you're asking me to marry you."

At that Pepper's vulnerability was supplanted by the sexy confidence that sent Alice's heart rate into the stratosphere. "Will you marry me, Alice Paul Cabot?"

"Only if you'll marry me back, Paddington."

"That's the way it works, generally. Yes, I will marry you back."

Striving to sound philosophical and composed, Alice observed, "It would be very efficient if we marry each other at the same time."

Laughing, Pepper turned the engine off and took out her phone. With the window down she took a picture of the museum, the diner, and the dusty road. "No one will believe this is where we decided to make it legal."

Maybe not, Alice thought. *But why not? Wasn't it places like this, where life, family, and love thrived in quiet and steadfast ways, that magic could happen?* "Hey."

"Hmm?"

She leaned across the center console to pull Pepper toward her.

"Oh," Pepper managed and then Alice kissed her, marveling at the vanilla sweetness of Pepper's lips and reveling in the quiet moan that was for Alice's ears only.

We're an *us*, Alice thought. We're *us*.

REFLECTIONS

(April, Also 4 Years Later)

"Is this some kind of April Fool's joke?" Helene felt it necessary to ask even though she was certain that Lauren would never participate in a mandated prank.

"No."

"Why did you bring me to my favorite restaurant to do this?" Aware of the woman two tables over taking their picture, Helene continued to smile as she said, "You know I don't yell, and I'd never throw the salad."

Lauren's smile was equally amiable and photogenic. "We've done this three times. I requested a table near the fire because I know how icy cold it's going to get."

Helene took one last look at the shoulders and biceps toned by decades of tennis. Funny that lust became nostalgia all in an instant. "You needn't have worried. Getting together again was a mistake. An occasionally fun but undoubted mistake."

She didn't need to add that she was aware that the many pictures Lauren had posted of the two of them at the holidays, Valentine's Day, skiing in Vail, and so on, had been meant to tweak Lauren's most recent ex.

On her part, it had meant a holiday season where she hadn't appeared to be alone. And there had been the satisfying sex—that had always been easy for them—even if less frequent than their earlier bouts of madness.

"I've been well aware you thought it was a mistake."

"Are you attempting to start a fight?" Helene made herself pick up the fork and appear to be enjoying her poached pear, goat cheese, and endive salad. "Why not *adieu, sans rancor*?"

"This time I feel how much of a waste it's all been."

She focused on how delectable and ripe the pear was. The white wine vinaigrette was tangy and fragrant with yuzu zest. She certainly cared more about that than whatever tired reasoning Lauren was about to unveil. "What 'it' are you referring to?"

"The charade."

"Was any of it a lie?" When Lauren didn't answer, Helene looked up from her fascination with the salad. Lauren's usually shining brown eyes were filled with hostility. "What lie have I told?"

"The lie is what we tell the world. Like the fact that I'm breaking up with you, and we're both smiling—so happy, so perfect."

"Darling, we're women. Famous, wealthy women. We both know there are people out there who hope to get rich by hating us. By destroying us. Every day a new reel about how ugly we are, or stupid, or fat. I don't plan to give them easy fodder for doing so."

"You tell yourself that now, but we both know the flawless presentation of a perfect life never started as protection. It was always selling a lie. Well, my life is far from perfect. Even when I'm with you, I'm alone. You glitter and shine like a diamond, so everyone wants to do that too. But they don't know the price is that on the inside you have to be as hard and cold as rocks."

The Châteauneuf-du-Pape she'd selected had more tannin than she found acceptable. Nevertheless, she swirled it in the glass before having another sip. "I'm definitely hearing that what we have is not what you want."

"What do we have? I can have a good time with a lot of people. So that part is not unique to us. What else do we have except this shared farce of happiness?" Lauren's smile began to fade as her eyes shone with tears. "I don't even have a close friend to talk to. I have to go deeper if I'm going to truly connect with other people. I'm afraid I've waited too long to even try."

Clearly, Lauren had to get through some script when it would be so much simpler to jump to the end of the scene. A perfectly delicious meal was going to go to waste. "So this isn't about me at all."

"Christ, Helene. Maybe I'm talking about me when I start a sentence with 'I have to.' You go ahead playing the perfect woman part. I need to be messy. Or I'll go crazy."

She heard a quiet ping from her phone. There didn't seem to be a reason to ignore it. "Excuse me, I have to make sure this isn't an emergency."

"Of course you do."

It took only a glance to absorb the gist of the message, and she tucked the phone back in her handbag. "Not an emergency."

Lauren's eyebrows were up as if she'd confirmed some obvious fact. "Was that from the assistant?"

"Which one?" She couldn't decide if she should pick up the wine again or have another bite of salad.

"You know which one I mean. You nearly smiled at it."

"I really don't know what you're talking about."

"You can lie to yourself, Helene. But I know you well. You've changed, almost as if you got your heart broke when she quit on you."

"It was never about that." *Damn.* It didn't look good that she'd confirmed Lauren was talking about Pepper Addington.

"Okay, not your heart. Your ego, though, absolutely. She's the one who turned you down."

"I ran afoul of prudishness."

Lauren's smile was suddenly wide and truly amused. "Tell yourself that. She made you feel ashamed of shopping for liaisons inside your office."

"This conversation is going nowhere." She brusquely waved at her plate when the server lingered.

"I think for the first time in your life there was someone whose good opinion and open adoration you really wanted. And that someone saw through to the ugly you've spackled out of sight with the likes of me. I'm not upset that we used each other."

"Then do tell me what is upsetting you."

"I'm upset at all the wasted time. Time I could have devoted to building real relationships with real people instead of a farce with *followers*. I finally figured out what my life has been missing, and I've spent too much of it pretending I already had it."

"Love? A picket fence? Sharing a cozy blanket while rewatching *Sex and the City*?"

"It's interesting that you think that's what love is about. I'm not even thinking about that. I'm connected to nothing and no one. I'm acknowledging that I don't want to go on living this way. I've actively denied it to myself. I chose to be an island that occasionally invited sex romps ashore, and now I don't see the upside of two decades living that way."

Clearly, Lauren had been back to therapy. The sculpted bronze body, gorgeous nails and hair, a voice that was listened to when anyone talked about women and sports—none of that was an upside for the hard work of maintaining a presence?

She reached into her handbag for her phone again. With a sad shake of the head and a glance at her watch, she said a little more loudly, "I'm sorry. I must get to the office. An emergency. You understand."

Lauren made a show of assuming a smile, but her eyes were brittle as papier-mâché. "I understand completely. Text me from the car, darling."

"I thought that was the last thing you wanted at this point," Helene snapped. With a jolt she realized her heart was pounding as if she cared about this very tired, predictable scene.

In the sweetest of tones, Lauren clarified, "Text me that you deleted me."

"Darling, your wish is my command. It's the first thing I'll take care of."

And it was.

The car interior was dark and welcome. Beyond a greeting, the driver knew she did not like to chat or listen to music. She preferred the white noise of the tires on asphalt. The driver's previous instructions had been to take her home and there was no reason to change that.

She hadn't expected to be alone, however. Of course she was most annoyed about the meal, which would have been exquisite, especially if she had requested a different wine.

The Los Angeles boulevard lights were reflected in yellow and neon orange across the car's windows. She'd expected Lauren to want to stop seeing each other at some point—she always did. Unexpected was that her reason was one Helene recognized. She desperately hoped that Lauren hadn't realized that.

It didn't matter who she was with, she was alone. Even Clarita, one of her earliest hires and a staunchly loyal right hand, wasn't a friend she could really share with.

Alone.

She reopened the message that Pepper had sent, still seeing nothing beyond a collegial sharing of a common interest. The Simply the Best compacts and lipstick cases were in fact worthy of collection and would stand the test of time for their beauty and design. Perhaps they should have a museum on the campus? Pity that she immediately knew the best person to put in charge of the idea was Pepper.

Such a charming, attractive woman. It remained a complete mystery why she'd prefer an unpleasant, barely fashionable, know-it-all journalist as a companion. The only time Pepper had disappointed Helene had been when she refused the offer of an intimate fling that would have led to a lifelong, supportive connection.

It was her ego Pepper had bruised—that's how Lauren saw it.

Lauren wasn't wrong. The surprise was that four years later the bruise was still there, even though she'd accepted the terms of Pepper's resignation. She knew that Pepper had been right— she had been fooling herself by thinking no one noticed she dated her assistants. The indulgence wasn't safe, even if it had always been mutually beneficial.

Of course, Pepper *had* been wrong that Helene would retaliate against her for the refusal. Pepper hadn't needed to quit, had she? No, of course not, and it really had not hurt Helene to tumble so hard off the pedestal she'd thought she was safely on.

That reporter girlfriend of hers likely thought Helene hated her. Hate was too strong. She did resent the incivil way the woman had pronounced judgment on Simply the Best's hiring, pay scales, and use of interns at a company all about lifting up women. She could still hear the sarcastic, "You may not know this, but paying women more money is a sure-fire way to empower them."

That didn't mean that Helene wasn't grateful to have a brand vulnerability pointed out, along with a way to fix it. All she had had to do was make the accusations not true.

It had even been easy.

So why was part of her hearing an increasingly loud inner voice asking, "What took you so long to do the right thing?"

Why am I required to always do the right thing? Men in her position weren't. The richer they got, the more impunity they enjoyed when they valued themselves more highly than literally any other thing on the planet, and that included the planet.

Her reflection in the window darkened the wrinkles that creased around her eyes when she was vexed. With a steadying breath, she resumed a serene expression before deliberately looking away. Home, and the basket containing a rose petal bath bomb and cucumber massage oil next to the whirlpool bathtub for two, was ten minutes away.

"Take me to the office."

The driver nodded and eased the long car over to make a U-turn.

She had no idea why she wanted to go to work. There likely would be no one in the building except security. The annual Composium was behind them, and the run up to May's traditional product line announcement was running smoothly.

She was still wondering why when she stumbled to a stop at the administrative building door. It had failed to whisk open. She needed her key card, she thought. *Of course.*

A startled security guard appeared from the rear of the first-floor lobby. She had almost reached the door by the time Helene had swiped her card. "Did you need something, ma'am?"

"Some forgotten paperwork," Helene demurred. She waved thanks and, as always, ran up the stairs to the second floor.

Even with the lighting low she was able to skirt the pendulum fountain showpiece. With no one to watch her, she trailed a fingertip along the bamboo and jute wallcovering. The nubby texture was one of her favorite things about the building. It did what she intended, reminding her of the natural world's infinite variation.

A moment later she cursed herself for putting the key card away. Of course she needed it to open the executive offices' main door and then again the door to her own office. The interior lights winked on as the lock clicked open.

As the door soundlessly closed behind her, her ears felt oddly tight, as if the office was hermetically sealed from the chaos of the outside world. Then a light fixture creaked for a moment as it warmed, and the feeling passed.

But there was nothing that met her gaze that would dispel the notion that she was the only person in existence at that moment. The carefully curated shelves of new merchandise designed to spur interest and conversation was its usual graceful perfection. The artful sculpture on the conference table, the soothing warm lights that bathed the commissioned wall hangings by local artists, the tactile cooling pleasure of her desk's glass top—it all reflected her style and elegance, by her own design.

There was not, and never had been, room for anyone else.

Her desk was not as she'd left it. A new folder had been set precisely at the left corner. She flipped it open to decide if it was worth sitting down to study. It was Clarita's summary of enclosed correspondence from an elite luxury cruise line that wanted to use only Simply the Best pampering products in their staterooms.

She closed it again with a sigh. Why was it so hard to find business partners with a modicum of vision? Why must she do it all? It was basic common sense not to limit the enhancement of their client experience to shampoo and hand lotion in the stateroom. Why not ask for exclusive scents, salts, and scrubs for their spa as well? Why not ask for onboard-only variations of STB best sellers? But no—not even the pedestrian collectability of a cruise-specific Simply the Best sisal and hemp tote bag with its certified organic and sustainable pedigree.

She stopped herself from flouncing into her chair. Instead she seated herself with care, pushed back sufficiently to cross her legs, and took a deep breath. After consulting her watch, and adding three hours for the East Coast, she picked up her mobile. She listened to the ring and swiveled around to face the floor-to-ceiling window behind her. At this hour the only thing she could see in the glass was herself. A navy-blue wrap dress that split over her creamy, lightly tanned legs. Red hair loose around her shoulders. The glitter of gold and bronze bangles and earrings in controlled and elegant disarray. Exactly right.

"Hello, Helene. Why are you calling so late?"

"I knew you'd still be up, *Maman*. I meant to call yesterday for your anniversary, but it was one of those days. How is *Papa*?"

"He's about the same as always. Weak, but steady. He remembers everything until about three o'clock. Doesn't talk a lot except under his breath."

"Not upset or frustrated?"

"No, never."

They chatted about weather and health until her mother's tiredness became obvious. "I will promise not to call again later if you get some regular sleep. Let the nurse make sure Papa gets to the bathroom if he gets up."

"I try, but I usually hear him. I don't need all that much sleep."

"When was the last time you had lunch out with a friend? Pat or Dorothy?"

"They don't like to come out this far anymore. Even though it's only a ten-minute drive from Hampton Bays station."

The image of her mother never leaving the big, cold house was distressing. "That's a pity. Don't forget that you can call the car service to go to them or have them brought to you. No need for the train. Did you write in your calendar that I'll see you in a couple of weeks? We'll go to the May Day Festival and enjoy fresh *oranjekoek*."

"That would be nice. I can't seem to find much enthusiasm for shopping these days, and the new cook is unimaginative."

Familiar with her mother's habitual dissatisfaction and the annual turnover among the estate's staff, Helene was still alarmed by the detachment in her mother's voice. The loneliness was palpable too. She was nearly eighty-one—was it all that unusual?

As Helene ended the call, she told herself she was *not* going to be her mother in another quarter century.

She laughed aloud. "Unless you're already her. *Merde*."

Lauren's words came back to her, about creating a lie for strangers to believe. It was also a lie for her to believe.

Merde.

She'd been selling the world on her perfect life for almost twenty years. Everywhere she looked she had crafted what was, to her, the epitome of taste and perfection. So why didn't the perfection make her feel complete the way it always had?

She looked at her reflection again. She was a jewel against the dark night. Rising from the chair, she stood with her nose almost on the glass.

What do you want?

Not this, she answered herself. If she continued the direction she was going, she'd arrive at a destination that did not interest her. If there was one thing she dreaded and had built her life around avoiding, it was boredom.

"Well, then," she said to the woman in the glass. "Perhaps it's time to do something…Something unexpected."

The woman in the glass lifted an eyebrow to ask, "What?"

"When I know, you'll know."

WILD THINGS

Published: 1996
Characters: Faith Fitzgerald, professor and historical biographer
Sydney Van Allen, lawyer and politician
Setting: Chicago, Illinois

The sixth is serendipity.

Previous *Frosting on the Cake* stories:
"Wild Things Are Free" in *Frosting 1*.
"Losing Faith" in *Frosting 2*.

HAVING FAITH

(May, 29 Years Later)

Vigorous quiet.
That's what Sydney Van Allen had told her staff and constituents she needed. It was the truth, and a more interesting way of saying, "I need to spend more time with my family."

It was a decision made eight months ago. For the first time in nearly three decades, her name would not be on a ballot. It was unsettling. Equally unsettling was the call she'd just concluded with a party representative to say, emphatically, that she did not want anyone's write-in vote.

"Everyone understands that you wanted to be with your father until he passed." The nasal-voiced operative had been making an effort to sound sympathetic, but the longer Sydney was out of the game the more clearly she saw the naked motives behind every interaction in the political sphere. "But now the way is clear for you—"

"I'm not interested in a return to the political life. I don't know how to say that more plainly."

"Come on, Syd. It's too much in your blood."

"It really isn't. I'd rather spend the rest of my days in the law and able to say what I think without measuring every syllable with a poll. I'd like to speak my mind and reap the whirlwind. There's always a whirlwind these days. So I might as well be honest."

"I'm going to keep asking, you know."

"I'll stop taking your calls."

The conversation had ended briefly thereafter. Her room, the one from her childhood and now decorated for an adult woman with a wife, returned to its former vigorously quiet state.

Quiet, that is, except for the repeated slams of vehicle doors in the front and rear yards of her parents'—her mother's, she corrected herself—expansive home. With only four hours until the arrival of first guests for the fundraiser this evening, the caterers were in a fever of activity.

It was going to be an all-star affair. Sydney had helped her mother with some of the legwork, identifying various notable personalities who would be willing to be named as co-chairs for a Planned Parenthood event. There was a large security detail patrolling the perimeter and grounds—every couple of minutes she heard a distant squawk of a radio as someone reported in.

"Syd? Look what I found in one of your dad's photo boxes."

She dropped her phone into her pocket and turned from the window to see Faith closing the bedroom door behind her. Her short hair was mussed where she tended to run her fingers through it, and she balanced a file box on her hip.

"Is it treasure?"

"A real memory lane trip."

"I thought we were going to tackle the picture project tomorrow, after the party."

"Yes, but you know me. I wanted to get a sense of a way forward. And we're going to need someone to scan them while we sort and cull."

Faith set the box on the wide desk that was finally a shared piece of furniture. Sydney realized that for all the years they'd been together, shared spaces had been covered with her briefings, her legislative drafts, her letters, her staffing reports, and on and on. Even if they'd been staying over for a single night, there had never been room for Faith's work on that desk.

Now Faith's tidy journals and trim laptop joined a short stack of books about Bavaria on the left side of the desk. Sydney's short reading pile of thrillers and biographies were stacked on the right.

Balance, Sydney thought. If their lives had been in balance a year ago, she would have been home when her father passed away instead of arriving three hours too late, delayed by some political thing that hadn't mattered a damn.

Faith lifted the lid from the sturdy file box. As expected, it was full of photographs in archival sleeves. On top was a photo of three people at an event nearly three decades earlier. As she handed it to Sydney, Faith murmured quietly, "It could be called 'A Study in Lies,' don't you think?"

Sydney studied each face. "No, not at all. Maybe 'A Confusion of Beginnings.' It's amazing that both of us looked so calm."

Faith eased it out of the archival sleeve. "I'm smiling at Eric even though I'd just met you, and I knew everything about my life was going to come undone."

"You're smiling at your date, that's true. I'm smiling at Eric, too, and I was telling myself I would never hurt him, that I could cope with you as my sister-in-law. Even though…"

Faith's arm slid around Sydney's waist as they gazed at the photograph together. Eric looked smashing in one of his flawless bespoke dark wool suits. Faith was lovely, as she always was to Sydney's eyes. She'd hardly changed over the years—smiling, kind, and serious.

A shimmer of desire ran through Sydney, as vivid as the memory of that night. Faith had seemed serene, with hair coiled into a charming bun at the nape of her neck and the curves of her body outlined by a simple little black cocktail dress.

One look and Sydney had imagined unzipping the dress, kissing her shoulders, and laying waste to a hotel room for a very long weekend.

She'd even known, in that glance, that Faith was not the kind of woman who disappeared for risky flings. Sydney had been determined to no longer be that kind of woman. When she became that woman she drank to the point of blackout. Or she drank to the point of blackout and became that woman.

Thirty-five years, seven months, two weeks, and three days.

"Even though what?"

Sydney ran her finger down Faith's image. "Even though you set every nerve in my body on fire."

"I wasn't trying to," she said honestly. "And the feeling was mutual."

"I know."

Faith's arm tightened around her. With a suggestive warmth, she asked, "Don't you have to shower before you get dressed for tonight?"

Sydney laughed. "We could lock the door and take our time."

"Why, Ms. Van Allen, in broad daylight?"

For answer, Sydney pulled Faith toward the bed. "Do you remember that first night?"

"When we fell asleep on the floor, after? Oh, to be young again."

She pushed Faith's hair back and cupped her face. "All my futures are with you."

Faith kissed her sweetly, then, with a little half gasp, more deeply. Familiar and magical, like always. There was so much beauty in their similar passions. She shrugged out of her sweater and felt Faith doing the same as they kissed. Shirts, bras, slacks, and socks all followed. They mutually tumbled onto the bed, briefly vying for who would be on top. Faith won. Her green eyes were alight with desire as she cupped and teased Sydney's breasts.

"Faith?"

"Mmm?" She bent lower to nuzzle at Sydney's earlobe.

"Did we lock the door?"

Her head shot up. "No. Um, be right back."

Sydney laughed as Faith hurried across the room and flipped the lock. When she turned around Sydney was right behind her. It was a delirious pleasure to push her against the door with something like the abandon of twenty-year-olds.

Faith's protest was half-hearted at best. "You cheated. I had the upper hand for once."

Her breasts brushed against Faith's and her knees wanted to buckle. "What was that about hands?"

"I—oh."

Damp curls slid apart as Sydney ran one lazy hand between Faith's legs. It was a wonder as always, as was the rising groan that was always Sydney's favorite music.

"Bed," Faith murmured. "Or I'll fall down. And then you'll fall down."

"So practical." Sydney let her go after another intimate, familiar caress.

With the covers thrown back, they glided together between the sheets, little words murmured between kisses. Then no words at all were shared back and forth until Sydney's quaking shout was quickly stifled by Faith's hand over her mouth. Moments later, if anyone had paused to determine the source of the sudden cry, all they would have heard then was laughter.

* * *

There's the orgasm and then there's the afterglow, Sydney thought. She focused her mind on where the hollow of her cheek rested on Faith's shoulder. She could hear her heartbeat slowing and feel Faith's deep sigh of pleasure. She'd just tasted, felt, and smelled love, and now she heard it and saw it in the flush that still covered Faith's chest.

How had she ever deserved this? Especially…

Her gaze went to the desk where Faith's interests and passions were now present as they'd never been before.

Faith ran her fingers through Sydney's hair. "We have about ten minutes, and then one of us needs to shower."

"Twenty if we shower together."

"You lecher. You know that never saves us time."

"You and your facts. So inconvenient." She made the wrenching sacrifice to peel her body away from Faith's and get out of bed. By the time she'd poured them both a glass of water from the carafe on the dresser, Faith was wrapped in her robe and watching the chaos in the courtyard below the window.

"Eric and Cinna are all over it. Thanks," Faith added as she accepted the glass and promptly drank it halfway to empty.

"Cinna and my mother are peas from the same pod."

After a noise of agreement, Faith asked, "How did the call go with that party operative?"

Leaving politics had slowed the noise in Sydney's head, which she welcomed. Maybe that was why she heard a note in Faith's voice. Uncertainty? Bracing herself? Had that note always been there when asking about Sydney's plans? And she'd never heard it before?

What is she afraid I'll say?

"I told him if he kept asking me to come back I'd stop taking his calls." As she spoke she turned to catch Faith's gaze.

"Really?"

"Really. Did you think I didn't mean it?"

"You're needed. You're necessary. You're a force of nature and—and you like the game."

"I won't change my mind. It's time for me to do something else. Rather, to be someone else."

Faith was listening intently and something in her eyes brightened, making them more blue than green. That light wasn't new, but Sydney realized then she hadn't seen it for a very, very long time. All at once Faith was the woman from the first night they'd met, her face full of dreams and vision and eyes fixed on a bright and determined future.

"Be someone else? How will you figure that out?"

Sydney lifted her shoulders in a genuine, baffled shrug. "Don't know. Time? Come on, let's shower. No friskies. My old lady bits are content."

"Heavens. I mean, so are mine."

A few minutes later, after scrubbing her face with the goo the dermatologist recommended, she asked Faith, "If you could go any place in the world tomorrow, where would it be?"

Faith's eyes were closed as she rinsed shampoo out of her hair. "The Bodleian Library."

"What's caught your research fancy that you want to visit that particular library—which I agree is rather cool."

"One of the Mauds. Actually, the mother of one of the many Mauds married to or fathered by or sister to a man with a title." She leaned back to let water run over her face, then brushed it out of her eyes. "I've been thinking about trying something new."

"Oh? For how long?"

"A while."

Which could mean years, Sydney knew. She gestured at the water. "I'm done if you are."

Faith turned the handle and leaned out of the shower for their towels. "That's what she said."

Sydney laughed outright. "Cheap, but true. That is what I said only ten minutes ago. Tell me about the something new you've been mulling over."

Faith threw the towel over her head and rubbed. From the muffled depths, Sydney heard, "I'm known for researched biographies with speculation."

"This is extremely true." Sydney made short work of toweling her own hair. She felt that what Faith was about to say was important and she didn't want to miss a nuance of it.

"But some women living in time periods I'd love to write about have a thimbleful of actual data. There's nothing left to discover about them that anyone can prove. So I've been thinking about fiction. Not speculation, but rather *invention* to fit what we do know."

Sydney immediately knew it was the right thing for Faith to try. "Wow—honey, I would read that."

"You don't think it's silly for me to do at my age?"

"What age is that? You've always been brilliant and somehow get better anyway." She padded out to the bedroom and stopped at the desk. "Be honest, how long have you been thinking about doing this?"

"I was thinking about it the most when we were at the fundraiser at that gorgeous house on the San Diego cliffs—

where they auctioned off the Beck sculpture for Planned Parenthood and that actress had that wardrobe malfunction."

"Oh, I do remember that."

"Who doesn't? Anyway, I was talking to a woman who wrote historical fiction epics. I'd read most of them—her research is impeccable."

That had to be nine or ten years ago, Sydney calculated. A decade of this dream put on hold. "Why didn't you pursue it?"

"It seemed unrealistic." The tiny "doesn't matter" shrug didn't ring true.

Over the drone of the hair dryer Faith was using, Sydney asked, "Why?"

"I didn't have the bandwidth it would take."

"Because you were busy being a political wife."

Faith opened her mouth to deny it, but Sydney quickly kissed her, which made Faith turn off the hair dryer.

"It was a full-time job, and you scarcely had time to write the biographies everyone loves." Sydney pulled her close, losing the towel along the way. *Oh darn.* "It's time to correct the scales the other way for a while. I can't think of anything better than London, libraries, and proper cuppas—and you. Us."

"Do you mean it, Syd?"

The careful excitement in Faith's voice was painful to hear. She wrapped both arms around this amazing woman. "I want you to go full speed ahead toward what *you* want. I will have your back. The only other priority is my mom."

"For me too."

They shared a soft kiss until Faith's still wet hair caused her to shiver and they set about the many steps required for donning formal wear. Sydney had promised her mother she wouldn't bring out one of her Lady Politician red jackets and a pair of black business slacks. Instead, she was shimmying into Spanx before doing an equally difficult shimmy into a close-fitting black sheath. What had she been thinking?

She caught sight of Faith shrugging into a champagne-colored floor-length gown that made magic with the curves of her shoulders and hips. "Darling, that's beautiful on you."

"Do you think so? I went shopping with your mother, and she picked it out and handled all the alterations."

"Elegant and classy, and I like what it does to your chesticle areas." She mimed their pleasing shape with her hands.

Faith looked down. "Well, they're attached to me. Might as well make the most of them."

"I'm totally in favor of that."

Her own toilette was much simpler than Faith's, but for her mother's sake she spent a few minutes with a mascara brush and eyeliner, then moved on to a lip brush.

Mouth stretched so that her upper lip was taut, she managed to ask, "Would you say that Henry was selfish with Eleanor of the Aquitaine's life?"

Faith was peering into the vanity mirror, a pair of tweezers in her hand. "Henry the Second? Her husband, not her son?"

"The husband."

"Yes, of course he was. He reeled in the wealthiest princess in Christendom who was already married to a king, claimed the incredibly wealthy Aquitaine as his own, and spent the rest of his life trying to keep her leashed. She dazzled him, but once they were married her needs were irrelevant. Then she kept raising armies to overthrow him, which made family gatherings interesting. Why do you ask?"

Sydney finished with the lip brush and surveyed the result. It was enough, especially after the effort of the dress. "You called me Henry, once. I think you were more correct than you knew at the time."

"How so?"

"I've been incredibly selfish with your life. You had a career and plans of your own, and they were never a priority in my mind." Sydney looked up at the rustle of Faith's gown as she rose from the vanity. Joining Sydney at the bathroom mirror, she met Sydney's reflected gaze.

"Don't do that," she said quietly. "Don't rob me of my agency. I *chose* to be who I've been all these years. You didn't cause it. Necessity didn't force me into anything. I could have chosen differently any time I wanted to. I didn't want to."

The fire in Faith's eyes was bright and humbling. "Okay. I hear you. It's not about me."

Her wife's lips curved in a patient smile. "Don't do that either, Syd. Of course it was about you. I love you. As confusing as it might be, both things can be true. Have been true. Will be true. It's not about you, and it's always about you."

Sydney was at a complete loss to think of any human being luckier than she was at that moment. The words felt inadequate, but she offered them anyway. "I'm going to do better at my version of that."

She followed Faith back to the vanity and watched as she leaned close to lightly dab foundation onto her cheeks.

"It's okay with me if you're a little more Henry from now on."

"Out of history that's not the model I'd go for. Not Eleanor either."

"Then who?"

Faith blinked at her in the mirror. "I don't honestly know."

"Do you want to find out?"

"Yes, I think I do."

Sydney went back to critiquing her appearance as Faith muttered the names of famous women through the ages under her breath.

This, she thought with satisfaction, *is going to be fun*.

PAINTED MOON

Published: 1994
Characters: Jackie Frakes, architect
Leah Beck, artist
Setting: Sierra Nevada Mountains and Bay Area, California

The fifth is for vision.

Previous *Frosting on the Cake* stories:
"Smudges" in *Frosting 1*.

"Living Canvas" originally appeared in *Painted Moon*'s twenty-fifth anniversary edition.

LIVING CANVAS

(June, 25 Years Later)

"That was a whirlwind, quite literally!" Jackie cast a last admiring glance at the sleek red-and-white helicopter as it lifted off from the Grand Marquis helipad. "I could get used to traveling that way."

"It helps to have a wealthy party host." Leah drew Jackie toward the rooftop doors of the hotel. "My stomach will need a little time to recover, though."

"What a glorious event that was. Are you pleased?" Jackie took one last look at the impossible, glittering dreamscape of LA's summer night skyline. She was partial to her own beloved San Francisco, even with Sales Force Tower redefining it, but Los Angeles was breathtaking in its own way—a profusion of white diamonds against black velvet. Directly below them, the cooling summer night breeze was stirring palm trees over the hotel's oversized pool and spa.

"That the sculpture inspired by and named after the love of my life"—Leah paused to smooch Jackie on the cheek—"raised over a quarter of a million for Planned Parenthood? Yes, I'm pleased."

The percussive whump-whump of another helicopter arriving matched the beat of the techno-dubstep pulsating from the hotel's top floor nightclub. It was a relief when they left the day's heat still rising from the roof for the air-conditioned confines of the hotel. "The whole night was thrilling—all those fantastic women in one place."

"Come dance with me," Leah said suddenly. She tugged on Jackie's arm. "We're all dressed up."

Suspecting they wouldn't last for even one song, Jackie was still happy to spend a few minutes swirling around a dance floor in Leah's arms. It didn't matter that they were the only people dancing. It was Thursday night and nearly everyone else was a male businessman looking exceedingly bored, tired, or both.

Jackie saw her amusement reflected in Leah's eyes. Two fifty-plus women in a posh neon nightclub definitely brought the Hip Factor down to zero. That they were dancing a bossa nova to high energy dubstep drove Hip Factor into negative numbers.

She didn't want the night to end, though. Leah's crystal, light, and paint creation *Jackie Saying Yes* had been wonderfully received at the fundraiser, and a bidding war between the tech millionaire host and an art broker had driven the price pleasingly high. The evening had been capped off by delectable food and wine and a speech from the Speaker of the House. They would have been put up in a swanky five-star hotel in posh seaside La Jolla if they hadn't needed to get back to Los Angeles for tomorrow morning's big event at UCLA.

Out of breath and pleasingly dizzy, Jackie relaxed into Leah's arms as the music segued from one ear-punching song to another.

"Let's go see how Georgia is doing," Leah shouted.

"I bet she's gone through all the popcorn."

Leah fanned herself on the way to the elevator and shucked off her dapper suit jacket. The enclosed space reminded Jackie via her nose that her silk caftan had to go directly to dry cleaning. She'd been so excited when the auction closed that her toast of celebration with Leah had sloshed wine back on herself. What a waste of an excellent Ardani vintage.

In the hallway on the way to their room, she checked her phone and showed a message from her mother to Leah. "She says congrats on the sale from both her and my dad."

Leah tipped her phone toward Jackie. "Same from Constance. She's all geared up for the gallery opening next week."

"*Peoples of This Earth* will be as phenomenal as the *Painted Moon* and the *Becoming, Dissolving* series were." Of this Jackie was absolutely certain.

Leah's agreement was guarded and her smile failed to light up her narrow face. "I wish I had your confidence."

If there was one thing Jackie had learned over the years, it was not to argue with Leah's doubts. They came with the territory of living with an artist. She'd experienced the same thing with her mother, and she knew something of them herself. Building designs could look dandy on paper, but it wasn't until people actually interacted with the space that she knew whether her concept was a success or failure. Waiting for feedback was sometimes excruciating.

She smelled popcorn as they approached their room. Georgia had definitely been snacking. What more could any teenager want? A hotel room, room service, a microwave, and high-speed Internet—heaven on earth.

Georgia's long, lanky body was sprawled across one of the beds. Two open textbooks were alongside her and a notebook was balanced across her knees. Dishes and glasses were on the table, along with a room service tray with a still neatly wrapped napkin and topped by an empty microwave popcorn bag. Another bag of popcorn, still half full, was next to her on the bed. "You guys are back already? Oh—I didn't realize how late it was."

Jackie surveyed the sprawl of the contents of Georgia's backpack across her bed, the table, and some of the floor. How did she do that, and so quickly? She gestured at the floor. "I gotta walk here."

"Sorry, Ema. I was going to clean up." Georgia paused *Captain Marvel* on the TV and wiped her buttery fingers on her jeans before gathering up some of her belongings and piling them haphazardly on her bed. She scooped the dishes from dinner onto the tray they'd been delivered on and covered it all with the fancy cloche. "How was the party?"

Jackie opened the door so that Georgia could set the tray in the hallway for pickup.

"The party was fabulous. Great food, really smart women—my favorite things." Leah loosened her tie with a deep sigh of relief. "Best part was this actress tripping, and I guess it's called a 'wardrobe malfunction.' Let's say there was nothing fake about her assets."

"Mom, are you objectifying her?" Georgia's outrage was palpable. "It totally sounds like you are objectifying her."

"I totally am."

"Gross!"

Leah laughed. "Made you say it."

"It could be worse." Jackie fiddled with the inner tie that pulled the caftan waist tight but couldn't get it loose. "We could be online looking for the pictures that people took instead of helping her up."

"Eww." Georgia flopped back on the bed.

Jackie said to Georgia, "And Mom's sculpture sold for two hundred and sixty thousand dollars. The auction was thrilling."

"That's a small-piece record!" Georgia gave another squeal as she bounded back to her feet to hug Leah.

Jackie was still grinning as she went into the bathroom for a quick shower. Georgia lived at the end of her feelings, completely contrary to what Leah called her "laconic" DNA. They had a long-running joke about both kids. Was this trait or that habit due to Leah's DNA? Or was it Jackie's surrogacy and nurturing? The intensity of the argument usually depended on how much trouble the child was in.

Regardless of whatever she and Leah agreed on, Jackie knew perfectly well where Georgia's forgetful squalor came from.

She'd seen Leah in the throes of creative passion too often not to trace that apple back to the mother tree. Happily, while a human being might fear to break Leah's concentration while she was working, Jackie had discovered that Leah didn't mind a dog leaning against her legs and whining for a walk. At which point, she'd suddenly realize the time and that she was hungry.

Even more happily, she never seemed to wonder how the door to her workshop had opened or why Jackie was outside it saying, "Good dog," and giving out treats. Unfortunately, they'd had to say goodbye to Butch the Second two months earlier. It was still a little too soon, but Jackie was keeping an eye out for Butch the Third. She missed having a dog in the house.

The tie on her caftan was now a knot. She stuck her head out into the main room, interrupting the ongoing debate between her daughter and Leah about *Wonder Woman* versus *Captain Marvel*—regarding which was more inspiring. Or feminist. Or had a better soundtrack.

"Seriously?" Georgia paused the movie. "Amazon costumes are so much better. Not a single bare midriff for boys to drool over, for starters."

"Captain Marvel doesn't have a bare midriff either."

"Yeah, but there's just one of her. They're an entire *island*."

Jackie interrupted with "I need help getting this thing off."

"Be right there." Leah turned back to Georgia as if to continue the argument.

Jackie loudly cleared her throat. "I'd like help now, please. Besides, you're not going to win on costumes, sorry. Amazons. In leather and boots. Ass kicking boots."

"I'm only playing devil's advocate. Be right back—I want to see the next scene." Leah joined Jackie in the bathroom. "How did she get so obsessed about movies?"

"I haven't a single clue." Jackie sneezed "Nature" into her hand and squealed when Leah tickled her.

"Sure. I'm not the one who bought the kids graphic novels when they were old enough not to eat them."

Jackie ignored the reminder. "If you pull down the zipper, you should be able to see the knot. I don't want the tie to snap."

Leah's lips brushed over the nape of Jackie's neck. "I promise to be gentle."

"Oh." A tingling shiver started in Jackie's spine, raising goose bumps on her shoulders and arms. "Don't start something you can't finish."

In the mirror she saw Leah glance at the closed door, then at the lock. She sighed. "Not quite enough privacy."

"And the movie is on pause. You've already been in here *for-eh-ver* in Georgia time." Her voice light and teasing, Jackie added, "You'll just have to wait."

Leah's arms swept around Jackie's body to cup her breasts as her teeth nipped at Jackie's earlobe. "So will you."

Now Jackie was eyeing the door and the lock. She groaned. "You know, life was easier when they were little and slept through the night."

Leah's narrow, dexterous fingers made short work of unraveling the knotted tie. "It was. But no, we had to go and feed them, and vaccinate them, and refuse to let them jump off cliffs even though all their friends were doing it."

"Mom," Georgia called, "are you done yet? I'm hitting Play in thirty seconds and you're going to miss the best part."

Jackie pushed Leah toward the bathroom door. "Go watch the best part."

Leah didn't budge. "That's what I want to do." She swooped in for a quick kiss. "All right, all right, I'm going."

She was rinsing shampoo out of her hair when the bathroom door opened again.

"Just me. I want to brush my teeth."

"Okay," Jackie answered.

A moment later a towel wiped a circle in the misted shower door and Leah peered at her. "This is the best part, oh yes it is."

Jackie flicked soap suds at her.

The ardent gleam in Leah's brown eyes morphed into innocent-puppy-dog shimmer. "What?"

"Not only have we already decided this is not the ideal location for shenanigans—"

Leah chortled. "Shenanigans?"

"We have to meet the parking shuttle at seven if we want a seat on the field instead of in the stands off to the side. That means ordering breakfast for six a.m."

"Oh, that."

Jackie closed her eyes for one last soak of her braid under the hot water. She didn't hear the shower door open, so she jumped slightly at the brush of a fingertip along the underside of her breast. "Stop that," she breathed.

"Something to remember me by."

"As if I could forget."

Leah blew her a kiss and left, taking with her the temptation to finish the shower together. Jackie thoroughly enjoyed the jangle of her nerves as she toweled off and pulled on an old, soft T-shirt for sleeping. All this time, and Leah could take her breath away as easily as she had the first weekend they met.

She joined in on watching the last few scenes of *Captain Marvel*, then savored the combination of cool luxurious sheets and Leah's warmth against her back. Within minutes the even, steady rhythm of Leah's breathing lulled her into sleep as well.

* * *

"Whose idea was this?" Georgia's baleful glare was directed at both of them.

"You'll get your turn in about five years," Leah reminded her daughter.

"Enjoy the cold while you can." Jackie wrapped a light scarf around her neck. "It'll be ninety by noon."

"And then I'll be fainting. *Dying*." Georgia trudged after them toward the waiting shuttle bus, where a queue of other families was forming. Parking in the remote lots of the Rose Bowl and taking a shuttle to the main gates was the best option when the closer lots were all closed for construction.

"If you faint or die, I expect you to walk it off." Leah increased her pace toward the shuttle bus as she snapped her waist pack into place. "Did you remember your water bottle?"

"Yes, Mom." Her boots scuffed loudly on the asphalt.

Leah rolled her eyes at Jackie, who turned her face so Georgia wouldn't see her smiling. Nobody could load a volume's worth of complaint, defiance, acceptance, and scorn into "Yes, Mom" the way Georgia could. That gift for inflection made her highly entertaining—when you weren't her mother.

The shuttle bus journey around the stadium maze was like Mr. Toad's Wild Ride. Every turn threw the passengers into each other, which Leah didn't mind when it was Jackie. Their bodies eased into each other, anticipating their matching balance. Easy and natural, like bonding silver with copper, making them both stronger and resilient.

Georgia, on the bench seat opposite, grumbled, "This is almost as bad as that sightseeing bus in Maracaibo."

"We can't see the road through the bottom of this bus," Jackie pointed out. "So we're doing okay."

"That was so much fun, though." Georgia's mood instantly lifted. "Gramma and Grampa are so adventurous. Kids at school don't believe me when I say they both ziplined."

Leah wasn't sure that her in-laws would ever do it again, but never say never with those two. Since Jackie's dad had retired from the diplomatic corps they'd been eco-touristing their way around the world, sending gifts to the kids from faraway places, and giving Jackie's mom ever-increasing inspiration for her art.

It was nothing short of a miracle to Leah that Jackie's parents had welcomed her into their lives and been jubilant at the arrival of not one but two grandchildren. Her own parents' disapproval and ostracism had never weakened, and Leah no longer invested energy in thoughts of reconciliation. They were missing out on Georgia, a ball of endless energy. Today, they wouldn't see Lin graduate.

They had never seen one of Georgia's drawings. They had never heard Lin sing.

Their loss. Their loss… She knew her life was filled with riches, but the sting of their rejection was still there after all these years.

She felt Jackie squeeze her hand and she met her love's steady gaze. It wouldn't surprise her if Jackie knew exactly what she was thinking. And was answering in her own mind, "I know, their loss. We have made our own home in spite of them."

A gift, every bit of it.

* * *

"Can you see him?" Leah strained onto her tiptoes, but the line of royal-blue gowns on the platform to the left of the main stage was a single mass at this distance. "I'm sorry I said this would be a good place. If only we'd known, we could have taken seats over there, closer to where he must be sitting."

"It'll be fine," Jackie soothed. "We can see the stage, which will be better than watching him wait for his turn. Plus a good view of the projection screen. Hey, we can tell people we've sat on the fifty-yard line at the Rose Bowl. But I'm going to remember this from now on whenever a movie has a battlefield of thousands and two people still spot each other from opposite sides."

"Legolas does it because he's got elf vision." Georgia, standing on her chair, was using Jackie's shoulder for balance. "I can't pick him out."

"My feet are soaked. I think they watered the field last night or something." Jackie glanced down at her sneakers. "But at least they're cool. The sun is incredibly bright."

"It does that." Georgia lightly hopped down to the ground. "Gets stuff hot, and shines light, and things like that."

"You're going to confuse me with all those science-y words."

Georgia consulted the program they'd been given at the entrance. "They should be starting any minute."

Leah glanced down at her own copy, but her eyes saw nothing beyond "Lin Frakes-Beck" in crisp charcoal letters against the pale ivory of the paper.

Jackie squeezed her arm in excitement. "I made sure my phone is completely charged. And Mom is capturing the livestream so we can watch again whenever we want."

Leah nodded, her throat too tight to speak. Would she ever be less nervous when the kids were in the spotlight? It's not as if they were anxious about it—it was just her. Lin was like a rock when it came to performing, rarely showing stage fright. In contrast, Georgia was always a bubble of nervous energy, but it seemed to make her even more confident under pressure. She wasn't a performer the same way her brother was, but she'd competed in spelling bees as a child and more recently in debates and poetry slams. Her energy level cranked automatically to eleven, and her nerves woke up her exceptional memory and quirky sense of humor.

Leah fought down a stomach that wanted to do flip-flops. Mostly because Lin was about to perform. And now that the big party was over, the gallery opening next week for *Peoples of This Earth* loomed larger and larger in her mind. She wouldn't be able to eat the day before, and the effort of shmoozing with critics and art dealers would leave her an exhausted wreck.

It was so hard to wait! How could Jackie sit there so calmly, when their son was about to sing to tens of thousands of people for UCLA's all-campus graduation event? It wasn't just kids and their families. There were Nobel laureates and actual rock stars in the audience. Very Famous People were there to watch their kid's graduation too. The freaking Dalai Lama was giving the main address. And in front of all those luminaries, their son was hoping to create an emotional exchange generated by pure, human electricity.

The official, decorous pronouncements from the Chancellor were followed by remarks from a string of invited alumni and the featured valedictorian. The sometimes slow pace failed to dull any of Leah's anxiety. Jackie knew her well enough to leave her alone, while Georgia ping-ponged as usual between extreme boredom and a fever of anticipation.

Finally, finally!

The Chancellor solemnly intoned, "A new tradition for this ceremony is the student-chosen *Song of Our Future*. Nearly eighty percent of the graduating seniors took part in the vote that chose the song. The performer was selected by the chairs of the four departments within our Herb Alpert School of Music, reflecting the student's academic qualities, objective performance measurement, and exceptional work ethic. Please welcome Lin Frakes-Beck, bachelor of arts candidate in ethnomusicology."

The first note, a low, long "oh" deep in Lin's chest, rolled out of the stadium speakers before the echo of the Chancellor's voice had died. Lin emerged from the left, the hum growing as the students reacted with cheers and applause. The hum rose into his tenor range and blossomed into the words, "Mercy, mercy, me." He repeated the phrase, and then played with it as he syncopated the rhythm with pats to his chest, a pattern the crowd closest to the stage quickly picked up.

He had told them about the honor of being chosen to perform but wouldn't tell them the song, only that he had never sung it for an audience before. Creating a performance piece had added to his workload during finals, but he took the challenge, "To see if I can, Mom."

Jackie was standing in the aisle next to her chair, turning slowly in a circle to video the audience's raised hands—ivory, russet, umber—washed over with golden sunlight. The sea of human colors was like a warm tide through Leah's heart. Her ears were filled with the shared claps pulsing against the white-hot syncopation of camera flashes. Georgia was joining the other kids, clapping along with her brother as he sang.

Leah could hardly breathe as she gazed at his narrow, lean face in the giant projection screen. The voice that flowed out of her son had to come from the anonymous donor, whose basic genetics and health had been chosen because they closely matched Jackie's. Under special interests it had only said, "Likes to sing, can play the violin."

It was more than the voice. It was the fire Lin fueled with blithe poise. She could see Jackie all over him, especially her effortless grace. She also saw her own father in Lin when he performed, something she hadn't told anyone. Her father had sung in church, and she had loved to hear him.

Idiotic bigotry—he could have heard his grandson sing today, if only he could have opened his heart.

Lin's gift could change the world; that's what art did, that's what music did.

That's what love did.

"Oh, mercy, mercy, me," he sang again, a lament for the overcrowded, sick planet written by Marvin Gaye nearly fifty years ago and what had changed? She wanted to cry, but then he turned it all around with a brilliant smile and lines she didn't recognize. Of his own creation?

We're not what they expect us to be,
Weaklings, haters, predators feeding on misery, no no
Whoa, mercy, mercy me,
Love will help us make history.

The song ended with a last, soft note and a final slap of his hand on his chest.

The crowd was on its feet, whooping and cheering. After a few seconds they began chanting something in unison.

Jackie stared at Leah, puzzled.

Georgia laughed and joined in. "*Yibambe!*"

Leah let out a delighted laugh. "Wakanda forever!"

"*Yibambe!*"

Leah shook her head. "The world is not ready for this generation—and thank goodness!"

As the Chancellor tried to quiet the crowd—with little initial success—Leah wondered if she had ever been this young. She must have been, she thought. She'd run away from college, from the Bible studies posing as art classes, completely rejecting her parents' idea of who she was supposed to be. She'd become her own kind of artist. Tilted at the stolid and unrelenting windmills of the art world. She must have thought she'd change the world back then.

Curious thought—did she still believe that was the case? Of course she did, or she wouldn't be creating. Looking at her kids and their generation all around her, she felt oddly reconnected to the self she'd forgotten. Maybe, just maybe, *Peoples of This Earth* would be okay.

When the applause finally died, Leah collapsed in her chair and heard Georgia saying, "I knew you'd cry, Mom," as she pushed a bundle of hotel tissues into her hand.

"It's just reaction," Leah muttered.

Jackie settled back into her chair. "That was brilliant! Brilliant! I'm so happy for him!"

The Dalai Lama began speaking, but it could have been Marvin the Martian for all that Leah heard.

Georgia looked as if she was about to burst. "I helped him with the new words he added, but it was a secret! I couldn't tell you. It's not like Marvin Gaye needed updating, but Lin wanted to connect the song to the idea that they're all graduating, and everybody has work to do, and part of that is not being a jerk to other people, and how we treat people is part of the reason why the planet is not getting any better." She paused for breath.

"It was perfect," Jackie said. "I'm so proud of you both."

A woman in front of them glanced over her shoulder with a pointed I'm-trying-listen-shut-up look, and Leah spent the rest of the ceremony holding Jackie's hand.

"I'm never going to live up to that," Georgia pronounced as they began the slow shuffle toward the exit.

"You don't have to. Be brilliant your own way, which is all that you can do, and no one can expect more than that," Jackie said. "You know what really matters."

"Be peaceful!" Georgia spun in a circle. "And love everyone!"

"Watch where you're going," Leah warned.

As Georgia apologized to the man she'd nearly trod on, Jackie's gaze met Leah's for a long, shared smile. "That was almost an out-of-body experience."

Leah's attention was lost in the stretch of their daughter's arm, the length of her leg, the balance of her weight. The sunlight beaming down on her dark hair. The shadow cast by her lashes across her cheeks. The image seared into her brain, and she stood, unblinking, until Jackie shook her gently.

"I got it," Jackie whispered in her ear.

"What?"

"Georgia. I felt you freeze. So I took her picture."

Leah was at a loss for words once again. Jackie's intimate awareness of her, and her innate kindness, still surprised her. These feelings and the image of Georgia might never stir to an artwork. But if they did, it would be the example of love in her life, in all its forms.

* * *

They didn't meet up with Lin until after his departmental ceremony late in the afternoon. Jackie had promised herself she wouldn't embarrass him in front of his friends, but when she spotted him on the steps in front of the School of Music pavilion, she completely lost it. Bawling like a baby, she didn't let go until she realized her tears were leaving blotches on his graduation gown.

"It's okay, Ema." Lin patted her back awkwardly.

"Sorry." She dabbed at her eyes with tissues.

"I expected Mom to cry, not you."

"You were splendid. I'm so proud of you."

He looked pleased as he shared a hug with a surprisingly dry-eyed Leah. Jackie wondered if Leah was spent of emotion after the morning's performance. She certainly felt spent now herself. She finished wiping the tears out of her eyes and studied her son. He was thinner, and his thick, curly brown hair needed to be cut. The soul patch he'd been cultivating at Spring Break was gone.

"Is that your diploma?" Georgia pointed at the rolled paper in his hand, tied neatly with blue and gold ribbons.

"Nah." He unfurled it for her benefit. "Instructions on how to get the real thing."

Leah gave him the no-nonsense mom stare. "Be sure to do that."

"Believe me, four years later, I'm getting the official sheepskin. Oh hey, does this make sense to you? I got a text from Grandma saying how much they liked the Marvin Gaye piece, and she said to show this picture to you."

He tipped his phone toward Leah, whose face relaxed into a broad smile.

Lin was saying, "An ad thanking some guy for giving money to Planned Parenthood? I don't get it."

Leah handed the phone to Jackie as she explained, "It's about last night's fundraiser."

It was indeed an ad consisting only of huge words against the newsprint, with "Planned Parenthood of Southern California" in the largest type of all. If Jackie scrolled around on the tiny screen it appeared to be a full page from the *Orange County Register*. "Well, that cost a pretty penny," she observed as she gave the phone back to Lin.

Leah explained, "Our party host told us the auction winner was a big name in family values in the area. He has one of those huge churches and buys art and cars with the collection plate money. Hates gay marriage but is with wife number three himself. And none of his followers seem to care as long as he hates the right people."

"The Internet tycoon ran up the price on him, too. That was delightful to watch," Jackie added. "All for women's health charities."

"Yes, she did, like it was Monopoly money. Anyhoo, looks like they're making sure everyone in the area knows his cash from the auction of my sculpture was donated to Planned Parenthood," Leah finished.

"That's subversive. I really like that." Lin's bronze-brown eyes, so like Leah's, gleamed with satisfaction.

"Do you have time for dinner or dessert?" Georgia sounded extremely solicitous of her brother's well-being for once, but a loud rumble from her stomach suggested she had other motives.

"I promised I'd meet up with the guys again later, but can we have dinner? I'm *starving*."

Jackie laughed because he sounded like the son she knew, and then she realized that the times when that happened would be less and less frequent every year. She fought back tears again. Wasn't this what she had wanted? Wasn't this a wonderful outcome of the adventure of their own family? Happy, healthy kids ready to take on the world? They had all that, and so much more.

As they walked across the central quad toward the parking shuttle area, Leah caught her hand and squeezed it. "What a beautiful evening, on top of an incredible day."

Jackie let her gaze roam over the jacaranda trees, their purple flutes giving way to bright buds of leaves. The archway they passed under was wound over with lavender wisteria casting shadows on the grass and sidewalks. A breeze tickled at the damp hair on the back of her neck, finally giving some relief from the heat of the day. Puff cotton clouds dotted the sky.

Ahead of them, Georgia was discussing her position in her last debate, and Lin was listening with at least an attempt at attention.

She nudged Leah with her shoulder and pointed at the horizon where the rolling Hollywood hills met the pale-blue sky. "The moon's rising. It'll be full and right overhead when the sun goes down. Do you ever think that the woman in the moon is smiling at us?" When she glanced back at Leah, she caught her breath. The long, taut gaze they shared was both memory and promise.

"Of course she is," Leah murmured.

She satisfied herself—for the moment—by kissing Leah's soft lips as she melted into her long, protective arms.

"Gross!" In case there was any chance they'd missed her meaning, Georgia added, "And super embarrassing."

"Busted," Leah murmured against her mouth.

"You're only encouraging them," Lin scolded. He crossed his arms and gave them a glare worthy of a Victorian nanny. "If you're *quite* finished?"

"Not a chance." Leah did let go of Jackie but still held her hands as they shared goofy, in-love smiles. "We're only getting started."

ROLLER COASTER

Published:	2011
Characters:	Laura Izmani, private caterer
	Helen Baynor, Broadway actress
	Cassidy Winters, Helen's agent
	Justin and Julie Browning, Helen's twins
Setting:	New York City, New York, and Woodside, California

Twenty-Five, and Many a Woman is Now Alive

HEARTLINE ROLL

(July, 14 Years Later)

Jolted awake by a skirl of Long Island Rail Road brakes, Helen sat up with a gasp.

Her wife, Laura, was already on her feet and reaching for her overnight bag in the rack over their heads. "We're coming into our stop, I think."

"Hampton Bays?"

"Yep. I'll get your bag."

Struggling to get to her feet as the train continued braking, Helen immediately said, "I can get it."

As if to make a liar of her, the train jolted one last time before stopping, forcing Helen to grab an overhead bar. Being right-handed, of course she used her right hand. That led to a pronounced wince and an under-the-breath curse that would have made the twins gleefully yell, "A buck in the swear jar! No exceptions."

"I've got them both," Laura repeated.

Helen spotted Laura's phone on her seat. Feeling at least partially useful, she grabbed it, carefully settled her handbag strap on her left shoulder, and followed Laura down the aisle. Passingly familiar with the wind and temperatures in the Hamptons, she peeled off the sweater that had made the train's air-conditioning tolerable. Sure enough, the platform was a wind tunnel, creating a searing, cough-inducing sirocco.

"Cheezits!" Laura exclaimed. "Now *that's* hot! I thought the city was bad."

Now that her rolling bag was on the ground, Helen took charge of it and handed back Laura's phone. Bursitis was no fun, no fun at all. "The city is worse. More smells you can't figure out and don't want to know where they come from anyway."

She was looking forward to two nights away from town. To be heading to a classic estate in the Hamptons wasn't the same as going home to her blissfully cool and beloved coastal California woods, but it was still a badly needed change. Being interviewed for the second time by the redoubtable Barbara Paul Cabot was a cherry on the sundae of life.

Helen had been fresh from her first Tony thirty-two years ago, but it was her work for a lower Manhattan AIDS charity that Barbara had wanted to talk about then. As an interviewer, Barbara was far less intrigued by what made people famous and more deeply fascinated by what they did with their fame. When she'd called in May to ask Helen to come out to one of her quarterly salon weekends, she'd explained it was part of a series of follow-ups.

"Be prepared for me to ask 'Whatever happened to...' more than once. Not a confrontation, but an exploration of the way life happens and how plans do and don't change."

"There've been plenty of fresh starts and lessons. We'll have a lot to talk about," Helen had assured her. Her husband's death was one of the ways life had happened. Realizing at the ripe age of fifty that she could love a woman with the same consuming, passionate, and sacred depth was another way life had happened.

Enterprising local ride drivers met the Friday afternoon trains at Hampton Bays. Within a minute they were ensconced in the back seat of a car with air-conditioning on full blast. It took only a few more minutes to reach the gates of the Cabot estate.

"I've made and served meals in a lot of rich and famous people's places." Laura was gazing at the four-story saltbox house with a pleased smile. "My favorites are still the ones that look like their history. Like coffee cake. Sure, it's old-fashioned and simple, but warm from the oven with a spoonful of whipped cream it's exactly as it should be and utterly perfect."

Helen caught the driver's eye in the rearview mirror and grinned. The young woman would have no idea that Laura saw the entire world through the prism of food. As they grew closer to the house, Helen had to agree with the comparison. Compared to some of the newer, opulent mansions that had been built out here, this one was simple and solid, with no fancy downspouts or filigree on the roofline. Coffee cake.

As they came to a stop in the expansive driveway circle, the tall front doors opened. "That's Barbara," Helen volunteered. "Known for her caftans."

Laura glanced at their approaching host while tapping at her phone to pay the driver. "As she should be—that color is fabulous. Like orange-grapefruit sorbet."

"Helen!" Barbara Cabot seemed to have the same energy she'd had thirty years ago. Her eyes, made larger by her black-rimmed glasses, were bright as ever, and the snow-white hair was as becoming as her long-ago brunette had been. "It's been far too long."

"Don't say that—you'll make us all feel very old."

"I am old." She held Helen at arm's length, studying her with her famously owlish gaze. "You, my dear, were born with fabulous genes, clearly."

"That and some minor but very skillfully placed injections. Theater is timeless, but I am not." She stepped back to draw Laura into the conversation. "I've also had the benefit of heaps of excellent food. This is my wife, Laura Izmani."

"Welcome to my home, Laura. I'm Barbara." They shook hands. "Don't worry about the luggage. Sophia will see to everything, which is what Sophia loves to do."

A tall, hawk-nosed woman with salt-and-pepper hair was already directing a young man in a plain black suit to a second-floor room.

"Come have some refreshments. It's beastly hot. If you need the powder room, it's just there," Barbara added with a wide gesture as they stepped into the soaring main hall. "We won't dress for dinner tonight, so please be comfortable. My daughter and her fiancée will be here later this evening."

Laura let out a pleased sigh. "I will be happy to thank Alice for the deep dive she did into molecular gastronomy and where the chemicals and food derivatives we all love to use are sourced around the world."

Barbara beamed with pride. "Science is her everything. This way. The sunroom is where the salon guests will gather tomorrow. It's where I live, for obvious reasons."

The long L-shaped room provided at least five areas for conversation clusters. One wall was crowded with photographs of their host with celebrities over the decades, and the others were graced with modern art that contrasted oranges and yellows against the creamy white walls. Helen followed Barbara toward a settee and two chairs with a low table in between. "My wife's food lingo has worn off on me, because I want to say this room is delicious. Perfectly seasoned."

"It truly is. Even when it's gray and cold out, I still come into this room most afternoons." She waved them toward the seating choices. "Wherever you like."

"I'd be hard to get out of this room too." Laura sat down beside Helen on the settee.

Barbara gestured at the silver tray with a cut glass pitcher beaded with condensation and several tall glasses filled with ice. "This is fresh lemonade. I can add something stronger if you'd like."

"Not for me," Helen said. "A little wine with dinner perhaps?"

"Sophia has picked out a delightful California red."

"Sounds perfect—and this lemonade will be perfect as is." Laura accepted her glass with a smile.

Helen took a grateful sip. "Lovely."

"Is that basil?" Laura asked after a healthy swallow. "It's very refreshing."

"Sophia's special recipe. Herbs are good for the liver. Or at least she's convinced they are."

Laura relaxed into the back of the settee, her long, lovely legs crossed at the ankle. "She's not wrong. Not that we should always think of food as medicine."

"You have my permission to share that wisdom with Sophia." Barbara turned to Helen. "Now. I have so many questions. I'll save most for tomorrow, but while we're alone and off-the-record, you must tell me how you two met."

"Julie needed a highly supervised diet. She's allergic to dyes, just for starters. When Laura came into our life as a private chef, life got so much better." Helen squeezed Laura's hand. "She was competent and compassionate. Always fun to talk to when I got home from New York every weekend. It took me a while to realize there was a lot more to how I felt than respect and friendship."

"For my part, I had figured it out before she did," Laura teased.

"Of course you did," Helen teased right back. "You knew you were lesbian, but I hadn't yet figured out I was bisexual."

Barbara's gaze traveled back and forth between them. "I will ask for more details tomorrow, about widowhood, being a single mother with a demanding career, and the magic of happiness found. Speaking of happiness, how *are* the twins? Thriving and healthy?"

"Justin is all about food—deeply influenced as a teenager by Laura's patient introduction to the art of making a salad. Since culinary school and an MBA, he's been doing private catering with Laura, and next week he'll be the new owner of Laura's fine dining catering business. Eventually he wants a restaurant of his own and is working his way into the scene."

"Believe me," Laura added, "I am ready to let go of catering."

"When I chatted with Helen she said something about a television job?"

"It's nothing consistent yet. I'll be making a few guest appearances here and there as a judge for several competition-style shows. It's fun, takes four to five days a month. Other days I can finally see if that collection of dye- and preservative-free recipes I've got can be made into a viable book. Maybe? Maybe not?"

Barbara rose to lift the pitcher and they both held out their glasses. "You won't know until you try, will you? Change is exciting." She topped up her own glass as well and sat down again. "The pandemic made me think it was time to fade into the twilight years. Then a friend reminded me I have a contact list that goes back decades and asked whyever didn't I use it?" Barbara glanced around the spacious room. "Tomorrow we'll have twenty interesting people. Good food, laughter, and Helen's interview. More food and laughter. It's very fun and nothing like I thought my twilight years would be, thank goodness."

Helen had been nodding as Barbara described it. "I know just what you mean about the twilight years. I'd be living them if it weren't for my agent, Cass Winters. She's a demon. After the years playing Mame I was ready to slow down a little, but not a lot."

"I too have a lot to be thankful to Cass for." Laura leaned into Helen. "TV gigs were not going to happen without her. The only downside is all that makeup. I really don't know how you do it."

It would be hard to explain how she actually liked the thick stage makeup—it was part of the transition into the character. "I don't think about it. It's a tool of the trade."

"In my early television years it was like Spackle," Barbara said. "The mascara would glue your eyes shut if you teared up. Can't have been that bad because I'm still here, but it wasn't fun. So Justin is on his way in life. What's new with your daughter?"

"She's the introvert to her brother's extrovert. Quietly passionate about everything. Design is her happy place. After Colombia and a turn at Parsons, she's in the Bay Area, focusing on digital art and curation in online spaces. I can't even begin to fathom what that means."

"Amazing, isn't it? You feed them, they grow, then off they go."

Laura gazed into her glass. "I miss feeding them. Sometimes."

"Sophia says the same thing. They go away, they come back. My Alice on occasion still brings home laundry, so there's that."

They chatted for a while longer and Laura excused herself to the powder room. It took Helen several minutes to wonder what was taking her so long. Another five passed before she finally said, "I wonder where Laura's gotten to?"

"Let's find her."

The moment they reached the entrance hallway again, Helen smelled a delectable blend of orange, black pepper, and garlic. "I know where she is."

"It's rather elementary, isn't it?" Barbara led the way between the curved stairs on each side of the hall that led to the second floor. The final door on the right proved to be the kitchen.

Laura was, indeed, in the kitchen, chatting a mile a minute with the formidable Sophia.

"I shake my head when cooking demos have the sauté oil turned so high that the moment anything is put in it oil spatters everywhere."

"You can tell that they don't do their own cleaning or else they'd learn." Sophia noted their arrival and continued stirring the contents of a heavy sauté pan that sizzled with garlic and onion. "We are fixing the world's problems. What have you been doing?"

Helen nodded at Laura. "I lost my wife, and we came looking."

Laura held up a bowl of finger-length baby carrots she'd peeled and trimmed. "I decided to be useful. Sophia has made us an upside-down peach caramel cake for dessert. That's after a ceviche of shrimp in Basque vinaigrette and clams linguine with wilted greens almondine and roasted carrots."

They had certainly fallen into the lap of pure luxury. "We're going to be spoiled."

To Barbara Sophia said, "I told her she didn't have to do the carrots, but she found the peeler on her own."

"I can't be idle in a kitchen. It's actually painful." Laura set the bowl of gleaming carrots on the counter near Sophia and brushed the peels off her cutting board into a compost container at the sink. "And now we should probably settle in."

Helen agreed. Her shoulder ached and she wanted to take a couple of ibuprofen.

Before showing them upstairs, Barbara toured them through the dining room, breakfast room, library, and the sitting room, where an impressively large television dominated.

"I like women's soccer and opera live from the Met. I don't like squinting. If you get bored after I've retired for the evening, feel free to pick a movie."

"You have quite a collection." Helen peered at the titles in the first of three shelves stuffed with DVDs and Blu-rays. Barbara's eclectic tastes were represented by *The Adventures of Buckaroo Banzai*, *The African Queen*, *At the Circus*, and many more.

Barbara left them at the door to their room, saying, "The WiFi code is amendmentnineteen, one word, all lower-case letters."

They quickly unpacked their toiletries and hung up their clothes, then Laura stretched out on the bed. "This is the good life. Come join me. I think I'm going to have a nap."

"Go ahead, you were up late last night." Their window looked out toward a tennis court and a densely wooded area. "I'll read for a while. Everyone is about to gather in the drawing room as the case is solved."

"Mm, sounds exciting."

Over the top of her book Helen watched Laura's eyes flutter closed. Laura's week had been exhausting as she wrapped up her final commitments as a fine dining caterer and officially sold The Food's the Thing to Justin and his equally eager business partner.

The quiet was lovely. The soft sound of turning pages was broken only by the little half laugh Laura let out when she turned onto her side. It never failed to make Helen smile.

A half hour later, Laura stirred. "Mm, have I overslept?"

"Dinner's still a ways off, I think."

She propped herself on her elbows. Over the years she'd kept her tightly kinked hair shaved close to her head, which meant she never had bedhead. Helen envied that. "Did the butler do it?"

"It was the butler's brother," Helen explained cheerfully. "Who was also the real father of the heiress and had been an operative for MI6 before taking up Thoroughbred breeding."

"That's a crazy English estate you got there."

"Don't get me started on the heiress's relationship to an American rancher who was a former Navy SEAL as well as baby daddy to the queen of influencers who was asked by the CIA to infiltrate Fashion Week."

"You're making me want to read it next. Though you also did spoil it for me."

"You asked."

Laura tipped her head to one side with a suggestive smile. "Why are you all the way over there?"

Helen sighed. "Because my shoulder hurts."

Laura rolled to her feet and stretched her back and arms. "The pills didn't help?"

"They did, a little, but I'm whiny, a little."

"Let's see if I can help." Stepping behind Helen's chair, Laura gently kneaded the nape of Helen's neck and across her shoulder blades.

"That's not where it hurts, but I love it."

"I was hoping to distract you."

Helen wanted to purr when Laura replaced her fingers with her lips. "You're very distracting. You always have been."

"Especially when I make oatmeal cookies?"

"That too."

A tap on the door ended the massage.

It was the young man who'd brought up their luggage. "Ms. Cabot asked me to let you know dinner is in five minutes. And to remind you it's casual."

* * *

Laura was not exaggerating when she said to Helen much later in the evening, "That was the best home-cooked meal I've ever had, including ones I made myself."

After dinner and an hour's conversation over dessert wine and fresh fruit, Barbara had retired to her room to make a few calls about tomorrow. Sophia had likewise turned in for the night, so they were taking advantage of a cooling breeze that had come in at sunset to take a walk along the terraced garden path that led down to the tennis court.

Their clasped hands swung between them as Helen agreed about the meal. "I'd say it was as good as meals you've made, because you are still the best cook I know."

"Flatterer."

"No, it's true. And I'm glad we're moving around."

"How's your shoulder?" Laura took the lead, picking their way through a stony part that wasn't as well-lit as the rest of the path. She had no desire for Helen to hurt any additional part of herself.

"I don't—hey, it doesn't hurt. Pills finally kicked in."

"Well, that's good news."

They reached the tennis court, walked all the way around it, and discovered a heavy wooden picnic table.

"There are lots of stars," Helen said. "Want to gaze for a while?"

"Sure." Laura scooted onto the tabletop and rested her feet on the bench. When Helen was settled next to her, she tipped her head back. "Do you know any of the constellations?"

"Orion. Which I don't see."

"Me neither. The stars are very pretty, though. And I like thinking that there are probably other people in the area looking up at the sky right at this moment, and they see the same thing we do."

"I like that thought. Want to make out?"

Laura laughed. "That's subtle."

"My shoulder doesn't hurt, and let's just say I've got more bandwidth for other parts of my body now."

Laura didn't need more light to know that Helen's vastly expressive eyes were alight with mischief and something more. "Okay."

Helen draped her arms on Laura's shoulders and pulled her close. The first kiss was full of smiles, then Helen sighed, and Laura relaxed into the moment. She cupped one hand to

Helen's cheek as they shared more deeply. It was wonderful to lose track of time. Her ears filled with the sound of their lips parting and Helen's ragged breathing as they kissed again. No clatter of pans, grind of blenders, or clank of a spatula on a grill. Just Helen and the sounds of the languid summer night.

That is, until she heard a woman's voice say, "Mom said they'd come down here. Oh! Uh, sorry…Don't let us interrupt."

Laura put a little distance between her face and Helen's. *Awkward.*

Helen, with the aplomb of someone who didn't let a fallen set piece stop the show, observed, "You must be Alice, Barbara's daughter."

Their arms were still around each other, and it seemed that Helen didn't want to change that. It took an effort, but Laura finally got her neck craned just right to see a tall, gangly woman in a tank top and shorts at the corner of the tennis court. Next to her, much more petite, was a bright-haired blonde with eyes like saucers.

Alice suggested, "Let's meet officially tomorrow, shall we?"

"Perhaps that would be best," Helen said.

"Carry on then." Alice was clearly enjoying the moment.

The blonde—Laura assumed she was Alice's fiancée—said nothing, but she had a starstruck smile Laura had seen directed at Helen many, many times.

"After you, Pepper."

Pepper didn't budge. "But I wanted—"

"Later."

"But, Alice…"

Just before they disappeared from sight, Pepper called over her shoulder, "I loved you in *Mame*!"

At that there was no stopping Laura's laughter. "Well, we've made a great first impression."

"I doubt we scarred them for life."

"Now where were we?"

"Here," Helen whispered. "Together."

MAYBE NEXT TIME

Published: 2003
Characters: Sabrina (Bree) Starling, violinist
Jorie Pukui, cultural anthropologist
Setting: Keauhou, Hawaii

Thirteen, a Baker's Dozen

TURTLES, ADAGIO

(August, 22 Years Later)

The sound of surf in her ears faded as Bree swam up from sleep and out of the Turtle Dance dream.

She didn't open her eyes, not yet. *Honumaoli*, grandmother of the waves, always welcomed Bree with strains of her mother's long, long-ago lullaby. They always swam side-by-side in blue water, cool at her feet, warmer at her fingertips reaching toward the sunlight above.

Her mother's voice was part of the water. *Your shell like a star in the sea, flying* honu *take me away, to where my true love will always be.*

Simple and sweet, and welcome.

Bree smiled into the night, her fingertips tracing the scars and tattoos on her left wrist. In the dream she always turned her face to the sun that lit up the sparkles of sand drifting in the waves. Swimming with the giant turtle was effortless. Honumaoli, her shell scarred with a century or more of life, was leading her to a gathering of angels. Bree's long, black hair drifted in the water, as did the flowing purple gown she was wearing, one much like the last she'd ever worn on a performance stage.

The dream had once been a nightmare. The sun would fade as she spiraled into darkness, and even her mother's voice couldn't reach her.

Slowly, year by year, it became a celebration of learning to dance even though she could no longer play her violin. As always, the heart-lifting, heart-breaking strains of "On the Nature of Daylight" rose in her. A song written shortly after she'd lost her ability to ever play it, it had once been too painful to listen to. Her right arm could bow the tight, climbing work of the melody, but her left hand would never press the strings hard enough again.

Was there music without sound?

The ache of desire for the violin to play her again eased as she joined the curving, graceful dance of the turtles. *Breathe, feel, love, let go.*

In the dream she no longer needed a violin to express the whirling, circling ecstasy of her lost voice. The music was there, and the patient kindness of the turtles, beloved honu, showed her almost nightly that she could still feel melody flow through her. She could experience pain and longing, loss and regret, and still be at peace.

A deep breath. The quiet sound of breath leaving her.

Some wounds never healed, but time allowed her to endure, to change, so that the place where hurt lived grew smaller, while love, and light, and purpose eclipsed it.

Love, especially love.

She opened her eyes.

She turned her head just enough to trace the silhouette of Jorie's head against the white pillowcase. The French doors that opened onto the balcony were ajar, letting in the sultry, muffled sounds of an August night, as well as a gentle *aniani* to riffle the curtains and cool her skin. She could hear the surf again, this time from the beach outside.

All the gods knew that the ocean and land were in endless conversation, and when combined with Jorie's steady breathing there was beauty beyond reason and description. Beauty that could only be felt.

The decades of always getting their love wrong had faded into the distant past, layered over, wave by wave, with the decades of getting it right. She wasn't sure that Jorie had kept track—there were now nearly as many good years as there had been years of loneliness, other people, and regrets.

She is music for a lifetime, her ancestors whispered. They came to her through her mother and had guided her well once she accepted that she could draw on their courage and hope. Composition and arrangement, guidance to gifted students, and guest lectures all combined to fill her days. She traveled often enough that a night like this, steeped in the simple peace and beauty of a lovely night at home, was a treasure.

Jorie smiled in her sleep, or so Bree thought, then she realized that Jorie's dark eyes were open. "Can't sleep?"

"I floated awake and here I am, watching you sleep and listening to the tide come in. I think I still have sand in my toes from our walk earlier."

"That's Island normal."

"As it should be." Her mind was still dancing in the blue ocean, but her body had other thoughts. Tomorrow would be hectic and busy. More sleep would be wise, but Jorie was meltingly soft in the moonlight.

"Come here," Jorie murmured.

She calls you, her ancestors whispered.

There was fire and the ocean, and Jorie was both at once. Her body was desired magic with the heat of mystery. Still a mystery, though Bree knew the curves and planes of it by touch and taste, from the lowest notes to the highest.

She moved on top of Jorie's welcoming warmth. Their kisses were sweet and rising in urgency. She whispered her lips over Jorie's eyebrows, her sienna skin, then moved easily downward to the tightening nipples she could feel against her own. She played her tongue over them and heard the first of Jorie's low moans.

Jorie's breathing grew ragged. Years of knowing made Bree bite down and they became deep ocean, rolling in unison until Jorie pushed her downward. "You know what I want."

She pulled Jorie's legs over her shoulders and breathed in the scent of desire. There was silk on her tongue. She drank, and she swam, encouraged by Jorie's hand behind her head. Through their physical connection she knew the violin had never been her only purpose. Another purpose was this, to love this woman, to be loved by her. To wring a sobbing groan from deep in Jorie's throat before she drew out a hoarse shout by going inside her.

Her left hand could play Jorie, could glide over skin and draw vibrato out of nerves. It was music of another kind, this woman's kind. Her face, her mouth, her hands were wet with the slippery desire that she loved. Then it was Jorie's hands that urged her faster and higher to the final climax.

"Come here." This time it was said with a satisfied sigh.

Bree settled against Jorie's side, the top of her head under Jorie's chin.

In the quiet of shared comfort, Jorie murmured, "You are so very good at that."

Bree laughed quietly against Jorie's shoulder. The surf still came to the shore, and every minute of their love had become as natural as the tide. "Thank you for all the practice hours and study, not to mention the instrument to play."

"Don't you sound smug? I suppose you've earned that." Jorie stretched her legs and shifted her pillow. "Is it terribly early?"

"Yes. Go back to sleep."

"It's the rules that *tutu* brings the mac salad so I can't sleep in. I also can't believe I'm the tutu."

"This is only the first of Penny's kids to graduate from high school. You get to be grandmother with mac salad two more times."

"At least one of those times Riki's mother will be the tutu who brings the mac salad. I'll be more than happy to roast the pig."

Bree couldn't stifle a yawn. "Maybe the two of you can work it out when it's not the middle of the night."

Jorie managed to reach the light sheet they'd pushed off the bed and pull it over them both. "You're lucky. You get to be Aunt Bree, bringer of bottled beverages."

"It's a good gig. And you know perfectly well that I would stir mac salad all day for Penny." Watching Jorie's daughter thrive as a weaving artist, teacher, wife, and mother had been satisfying—a life Bree had never wanted but nevertheless cheered because it was everything Penny had dreamed for herself. "She reminds me so much of your mom."

"Her ancestors are strong."

A few minutes later, Jorie's breathing slowed and resumed the steady, deep rhythm that was part of Bree's nights. It blended with the waves rustling onto the sand, and together they washed away the last of the music from her dream.

Moving carefully, she slipped out of bed, found her muumuu, and curled up in her favorite living room chair. Her music player and headphones were always waiting for her. The Barber *Adagio*? Tallis *Fantasia*? She could listen to her performance of them now without distress. The music the violin had made with her was nevertheless alive. Goldberg *Variations*? Vivaldi's "Winter"? The new arrangement of her "Ahe Honi" performed for the concert to help rebuild Lahaina?

Milimili keiki, our little one. Her mother's voice joined with all her ancestors, then fell quiet.

It was a velvet night. A kindly island breeze kissed her bare legs. The sound of the darkness was full of Jorie's breath, the creak of the land, and hiss of water on sand and rock. There—in the distance, the hooting call of the *pueo*.

Iz, she thought. For a night like this, the tender voice of the gentle giant was perfect. She visualized the ukulele and the finger-holds that would draw "Somewhere Over the Rainbow" and "What a Wonderful World" from such strangely tuned strings. Her right hand strummed the arm of the chair, and it did not hurt at all for her left to approximate the fingering.

Tomorrow there would be sun and her *'ohana*, the blue ocean, and her dancing turtles. Every moment she was given would hold these gifts. She was already over the rainbow and no longer had anything to fear from the dark, sacred night.

ABOVE TEMPTATION

Published: 2010
Characters: Kip Barrett, private fraud investigator
Tamara Sterling, owner Sterling Fraud Investigations
Setting: Seattle and Puget Sound, Washington

Squee! O Glee! We are twenty-three!

Previous *Frosting on the Cake* stories:
"Snap Judgment" in *Frosting 2*.

KINDLING

(September, 15 Years Later)

Tam tried not to spill any of her hot coffee as she hurried to the cabin's ground floor bay window. She wasn't entirely successful, but she didn't want to miss it. The moment that she'd surfaced out of an exhausted sleep she'd realized what the steady *crunch-thunk* had to be.

Kip was chopping wood.

A lovely sight it was. In spite of the frosty late September temperatures of the deep forest off Puget Sound, Kip wore a tank top and jeans. Her petite frame was a study in muscles and circular motion as she lifted the axe, arced it on her right side around calf, hip, shoulder, overhead, and then down. Logs split with a satisfying crack. Energy, purpose, drive—that was Kip in a nutshell.

The steady sound of the axe falling on wood was the only sound aside from the low hum of the refrigerator and the muted crackle of the fire in the large wood stove that heated the cabin and cooked all their meals. After leaving behind the ninety-degree weather in Seattle just across the Sound, the fifty-degree chill was proving a shock to Tam's system. Yet there was Kip, breath misting in the air as she worked, reveling in it.

The cabin's remote location in the lee of the Olympic Mountains was its biggest appeal, especially when they both were so badly in need of a break. A bruising summer and fall of endless travel and stress had dealt them nonstop setbacks and challenges. For Tam, it was coping, badly, with a legal system that could no longer be counted on as an ally in prosecuting financial fraud.

Last week she'd run into Mercedes Houston, her former assistant and now Sterling Fraud Investigations' VP of Operations. It had been some time since their paths had overlapped. Mercedes had lured Tam to her nearby office with the promise of genuine Kona coffee. Her office door had scarcely closed before Mercedes picked up on their last conversation as if it had never ended.

"When are you going to get a life? How much weight have you lost? What do you think is going to happen if you take a real vacation? A *long* vacation?"

She'd made the usual excuses, said "Yes, but..." several times, and finally yielded up a weak-ass promise that she'd *try*. Mercedes's exasperated sigh told Tam how much faith she put in it.

What do you think is going to happen if you take a real vacation?

That was an easy answer. There'd be one less voice pushing back against an unraveling judicial system that preferred to fine companies for fraud instead of jailing the people who'd made the fraudulent decisions. It was harder than ever to get convictions and damage payouts that would deter future, repeating behavior. Openly shop your case to a judge who thought wealth was the same as the law, delay every possible step of the way, and walk free when prosecutors simply couldn't keep going anymore.

She was exhausted. Prosecutors were exhausted. Judges were exhausted with no relief to overburdened dockets in sight.

Kip, for her part, was neck-deep in the new Wild West of cryptocurrency, where lack of regulation made all the usual forms of theft very popular. There were also brand-new ways to steal, including some that the law didn't even cover yet when actual cash hadn't changed hands.

Kip's axe continued to rise and fall with satisfying results. Tam supposed she ought to get dressed and offer to stack the wood.

Later. When her working woman came in, having fresh coffee and something to eat ready would be more welcome.

Where did Kip get the energy? What had begun as a solo career doing independent, private financial audits for big-name entertainers had become a small firm with like-minded analysts and investigators. Their client list was star-studded. Tam envied Kip a certain "Fuck the Patriarchy" friendship bracelet, that was for sure.

Kip leaned on the axe and glanced back at the cabin. Tam waved and wasn't sure Kip could see her until Kip blew back a kiss. With a deep breath she let all her love for Kip well up. No reason to put it away to focus on work. They didn't have to go back across the Sound until tomorrow night.

With that thought something in her chest twisted. She winced and forced herself to take a very deep breath. The pleasure of the morning fled, and the thought echoed in her head—the one she'd been ignoring for far too long.

Do. The. Math.

Tomorrow night was forty-eight hours at the cabin with three-hour drives on each end. Fifty-four hours together, just them.

Fifty-four hours was the most continuous time they'd spent together over the past eleven months.

She didn't want to do the math. The math sucked.

One reason they were both good at their jobs was that compartmentalizing came easily. They were productive in their work and equally able to set work and worry aside when they had time together.

Tam knew perfectly well that they should be counting time together by the day and week and month and year and decade. Not by the hour.

It was pointless, however, to make promises neither of them could keep, like having an unbreakable date night or dedicated no-travel week together at least once a quarter. They relied on the fact that when they did have time together they made the most of it.

"And we lie to ourselves that it's enough," Tam whispered aloud. She knew it was a lie—did Kip? Every time she wanted to bring it up, she stopped herself because there was no way out. A court case that was too important. Data gathering on criminal acts was done at a breakneck, relentless pace—the work mattered.

But don't we matter too?

Like last night. It had been not much above freezing inside when they'd arrived. Within minutes Kip had kicked on the generator and started a fire while Tam stowed the groceries. Minutes after that they'd been in bed, and the cold sheets hadn't mattered. When they wanted it to, the world went away.

Tam could still feel Kip's touch and kisses, and her body was so content she didn't want to do anything that would shake off the afterglow. The coffee was cooling, and she hadn't yet taken a sip. She could still taste Kip on her lips and coffee would take that away. She wanted to be wrapped in the best kind of tired.

Kip had risen early, that was clear, and every log she split was probably the face of the venue manager who'd casually inserted outlandish language into a venue contract that none of Kip's clients had read before signing. The new clause stated that the folk-rock trio would be paid in the cryptocurrency of the venue's choosing. This created cash flow and tax problems for the musicians, who were, in turn, required to pay their roadies, transit workers, and staff with actual cash. The IRS expected cash as well. That's when Kip had entered the equation as a referral from another musical act.

Undisclosed, of course, was that the venue manager was getting bounties for every band he signed up for the cryptocurrency. The bounties were significant, which, to both of their trained eyes, meant something was sketchy. As soon as Kip had looked up the founder and taken note of the guy's lavish spending and constant marketing of his currency as a "system" versus an "asset," Kip had initiated a withdrawal of all of it.

Yesterday the mastermind dudebro himself had called Kip personally to berate her for not understanding how his system would make her clients rich. Eventually. But no guarantees. She'd told him to cash out the money anyway.

Last night in the car Kip had laid it all out, and they'd gleefully discussed the documentation memo Kip could forward to friends she still had at the SEC. In the meantime, her top priority was cashing out the crypto and getting it into a bank before anyone filed complaints with their union. It had been fun, talking over the problem, pulling at different angles—they thought in similar patterns. It had been so welcome an exchange that Tam had let go of her plan to bring up what she thought of as The Time-Math Conundrum.

It wasn't that they didn't love each other. Tam had no doubt about that. However, why bring up a problem that couldn't be fixed? Why talk about it when nothing would change?

The coffee was stone-cold now. Watching Kip was a rare treat and would be over too soon. *And here I am again, thinking about how many hours it is until we leave.*

She could hear the scoffing of her inner critic, the one that sounded like her favorite courtroom prosecutors. "When was it you decided that you were powerless to change the situation?"

When had it happened? After their first year of fighting for time they'd slowly given in to the real urgency and stakes of the work they both did very well. Success was a trap, she thought suddenly. That was what this mood felt like—a trap. A doom loop. There's never enough time to talk it through with Kip, to make any changes they could both live with, and therefore she'd accepted there was no way out. Lather. Rinse. Repeat, repeat, repeat.

She watched Kip take a break, chest heaving, hands on hips, and head lifted as if to hear the seventy-foot pines sway in the chilly wind coming down off the Olympic mountains. They were secluded in a world ringed by poplar with leaves long turned red, dusky green evergreen fir, and thin, knotty pine. Overhead was a soft blue sky and long, fast-moving white clouds so thin they hardly blocked the brilliant morning sun.

A dozen more logs were split before it looked like Kip was nearly done. Pulling her robe close, Tam ground more beans from their favorite Pikes Market roaster and poured over hot water from the kettle that was a permanent fixture on the top of the old-fashioned wood stove. Kip deserved fresh coffee, and Tam could warm up her own to a drinkable temperature when the filter stopped dripping.

She wasn't as used to the simple life at the cabin as Kip was—it had been Kip's hideaway spot, inherited from her beloved grandfather. It was with some pride, then, that she greeted Kip with bagels split and toasted on the stove top, then spread with cream cheese and covered with strips of smoked salmon and a few capers. The simple life was simpler if you'd stopped at a really good grocery along the way.

"You are a prince among women." Kip accepted the kitchen towel Tam handed her, mopped at her ruddy face before running it over her short, damp hair. Without ceremony, she took a large bite out of a bagel. "I'm beyond hungry."

"You've earned it. That was impressive."

She got a cream-cheesy smooch. "Fresh coffee?"

"Of course."

Plopped down at the small table halfway between the sink and the stove, Kip said, "The air outside is like wine. I feel so much better already."

"That makes me very happy."

"I'm going to snarf up the food and then get in the shower. There should be hot water by now."

"There is—I thought I should wash my hands before making breakfast. Because, well…"

Kip blushed, which was adorable because she didn't blush for anyone but Tam. Most people who knew her would probably say Kip was stone-faced and unreadable. "Yes, well. They were busy last night."

"I slept hard."

"Me too." Tam opened her mouth to bring up The Time-Math Conundrum, then only said, "We're both so tired."

Coward.

Well, what was the point of beginning a painful discussion when they had to go back to Seattle tomorrow night and Kip was licking cream cheese off her thumb?

"Maybe I should join you in that shower. Save water."

"How ecologically minded of you."

"I'm all about the planet." She dropped the joking air. "And your delicious body."

Kip swallowed hard. "I did bring a new shower gel."

Kip in a robe was adorable. Kip out of a robe was powerfully compact proof of the adage that very, very good things could come in small packages. The water was hot, but Tam still broke out in goosebumps when Kip massaged her shoulders and back with her strong, sensitive hands. It was the best shower she'd had in a very long time.

Even better, after the shower, Kip was eager to find a dry and horizontal position for further attentions to Tam's body.

It wasn't even noon. She was in a warm bed. Kip's hair was tickling her nose. Her cell phone didn't get a signal. With a deep breath she inhaled the smell of the wood fire, the citrusy scent of the new shower gel, and the damp mist left over from the shower. Now to exhale the nonstop stress of daily life.

She closed her eyes and was back in the Bahamas fifteen years ago, on the day Kip had said "I love you." How she'd looked—brave and scared and adamant. There had been a stark truth in their situation, simply that there was no way in heaven or hell that if they spent another night in each other's company they wouldn't give into the burning attraction that distracted them both.

No one would have known but them.

Unfortunately, they both believed that rules are rules even when no one is watching, and Sterling Fraud Investigations had a strict policy about employee fraternization—a policy Tam had written herself. Fraternization when discovered led to accusations of unfitness, impaired judgment, flawed work ethic—all of which led to compromised court cases.

Kip had been the one to find the way around the rule. They'd successfully recovered stolen funds, sent two thieves to jail, and cleared both their names. That day, with the scent of fruit and the ocean in the wind, Kip had said the words that sealed their relationship. Not "I love you," though that mattered. What changed everything was "I quit."

She blinked as The Time-Math Conundrum solved itself in her head. She hadn't questioned the Conundrum's underlying assumptions, some of them dating back fifteen years.

In those years, Sterling Fraud Investigations had grown, reorganized, merged with smaller firms, and opened two new offices. By the end of the year another merger would be completed, bringing a welcome influx of energy.

Well, hell. Mercedes Houston had been right all along. Tam needed to take a *long* vacation. A permanent vacation.

She really was an idiot to have taken so long to figure it out. Mountain air and Kip had finally let her brain accept that the world would indeed keep on turning if Tamara Sterling retired.

She waited until Kip stirred and they shared sleepy kisses.

"I have something to tell you, and it's going to come as a surprise."

Kip's eyes opened. "Go for it."

She traced the line of Kip's upper lip and smiled when Kip nibbled at her fingertip. "I quit," she said all in a rush.

"You don't smoke. You don't really drink much. Caffeine?"

"No—"

"Please don't say it's chocolate." Kip's eyes unfocused as she seemed to contemplate a horror almost beyond words. "Or cheese."

"I'm quitting Sterling. Retiring as CEO. It's the only solution."

Kip sat up straight and pulled the covers to her shoulders before asking, "Solution to what?"

"The lack of time for us—for anything but work. You want to spend more time together, don't you?"

"Yes, of course, but our schedules—"

"Exactly." Tam scooted up to join Kip in leaning against the headboard, carefully keeping the blankets close to hold in the warmth. "I can't go on not being in the same bed with you more than half the nights of the year. Or finding fifty hours to spend together every eleven months. It's the job or us."

"Are you worried?" Kip bit her lower lip. "About us? Why would you be worried about us?"

"I'm worried about this treadmill we've been on—it's good work, don't get me wrong. I still believe in truth and justice and catching bad guys. But I don't want to spend another fifteen years not waking up with you. The world will go on."

Kip had cocked her head to one side as Tam grew more passionate. "You know, I thought it was just me. Wishing we weren't quite so devoted to our work. But every time I thought that, I felt as if I were betraying something. Though I'm not sure what."

Tam slipped one arm around Kip to better breathe her in. "Fifteen years ago you upended your entire life to choose me. To give us a chance. It won't cost me nearly as much to choose you—and besides, it simply feels like time for me to let go and maybe grow into something else. I'm going to be the big six-oh in just a few short years."

"Are you sure?" Kip looked up from Tam's shoulder. "Very sure?"

"Yes. Absolutely sure. As sure as you were."

"I—I'm going to have to get used to the idea. Not because I don't want more weekends like this. Not more. I want every weekend like this. I want *weekends*."

That surprised Tam. "You're saying *you* want to scale back? I wasn't going to ask you to do that. I know you enjoy it."

Kip narrowed her gaze. "You know why I worked long hours? I mean, continued to long after it was necessary to keep the firm running?"

Tam considered the question. "One minute ago I would have said it was devotion to the principles of fairness and justice, but right now I'm pretty sure that's not the whole story."

"I worked long hours because you did, silly. Why sit at home waiting? I was afraid it would make me bitter and clingy—and you did not need that from me."

Tam laughed as she shook her head. "It seems very clear to me that we should talk more often."

Kip tickled her in response.

After a brief tussle and several kisses, Kip nudged Tam with her shoulder. "We should get dressed and talk more."

"I love talking here." Tam traced the curve of Kip's ribs with the palm of her hand.

"I do too, but there's no lunch here, and I'm hungry."

"Have I told you lately how much I adore you for liking food the way you do?"

"No, you haven't, so thank you." Kip made no move to leave the warmth of the bed, however. "How can you just…quit?"

"The merger with Integrity. It was a long time getting it to happen, and now I see that I'm superfluous."

"No, you're not. Your name's on the company."

"Okay then. Let's say that I'm no longer essential. We're changing our whole org chart and what better time to replace me? There are a lot of very talented people coming on board, and Hank will make a great CEO. A couple of years ago he seriously considered moving out of New York to Seattle but didn't want to make all that change for a lateral transfer. This would be a promotion."

"It's always been your life. After you left the FBI, I mean." Kip snuggled a little closer.

"It was. Just like it was your life—until it wasn't. Leaving didn't break you, and it won't break me. Do you know how long it's been since I went to a play?"

"Not since we've been together. And neither have I."

"Do we like the theater?"

Kip grinned. "I have no idea. But I'd like to find out."

Tam rubbed her calf against Kip's. Strong and soft at the same time. "We could travel places together just to go there."

"You mean, like, uh, what's that called? Vacations?"

Tam smooched her. "That's the word: *vacations*. I've seen so little of the world outside of office parks and skyscrapers. I'd love to visit Argentina and Australia and Alsace and the Arctic Circle. Then we can start on the B's. All with you."

"Blue Ridge Mountains, Barcelona, Belfast. Your turn."

Once upon a time she'd thought Kip was dull and humorless. First impressions were sometimes completely wrong. "Canada. All of it."

"That'll take a while. So we'll have vacations. This is good." Kip was nodding happily.

Tam kissed Kip's shoulder. "We can make this work."

"Have you thought of what else you'd want to do?"

"Not until this very moment. But you know what we were talking about on the drive? The way venue operators are using crypto more and more?"

"Sure. Like how we can't even figure out if it was defrauding behavior for that venue to arbitrage the ticket pricing using faster than speed of light buys and sells in crypto before the purchase was even credited by a bank, and none of that leveraging was shared with the artist?"

"Like that. Just like that. I think I want to dig into policy with this law firm in Redmond that's been taking on legislative consulting. They asked and I was going to turn them down. But it's what I should do. Right now legal policy on currency, artificial intelligence, and accountability is so far behind what's coming. Hell, it's far behind what already exists. It's the same old crimes, fraud and money laundering, with brand new tools. Scary tools."

"With the same old excuses—it's the tool that did it, not me."

They sighed in unison.

Kip turned her head to meet Tam's gaze again. With a tender smile, she said, "I didn't think I could love you more."

"I'm going to try to make you say that again and again. I want to share the life we dreamed about but never made happen—so we stopped dreaming about it."

"It doesn't have to be perfect. As long as we're together."

Tam pulled Kip as close as she possibly could. "This will be messy, but I think I can be out in a couple of months or less. There's one case to see through to the end, and the others are early enough that I can hand them off. After that it's introducing the new CEO to clients. Hand holding."

"But it could take longer. I understand." Kip's stomach growled and moments later she was out of the bed and scrambling into a thick sweatshirt.

The bed instantly grew colder, so Tam abandoned it as well. From inside her T-shirt she said, "Don't be so understanding. Keep me motivated. Badger me like Mercedes would."

"Not my style." Kip hopped from one foot to the other to pull on socks. "Well, nobody has Mercedes's style."

Tam's shivers subsided when she zipped up her jeans and zipped up a fleece hoodie. "Mercedes will be happy. In between wishing us well, she'll be saying 'I told you so.'"

"She will?" Kip turned to watch Tam get dressed.

"Well, she told me to do this ten years ago. Something about the world not devolving into endless criminality if I decided to do something else with my life. And you deserving more than the crappy life I was supposedly sharing with you."

"Here." Kip tossed her a beanie and Tam gratefully pulled it down far enough to cover the tips of her ears.

"We're going to get another heat source into this cabin."

"Why do you think I was chopping wood? The fire in the stove is probably down to nothing."

"I approve of getting that fire going as hot as we can."

Kip winked at her and led the way downstairs. "Mercedes was wrong, you know. Our life never was and isn't crappy." Kip froze with one hand on the banister. "Don't you dare tell Mercedes I said she was wrong."

"Honey, I would never do that to you."

In the kitchen Kip put her hand on the kettle and quickly snatched it away. "We've got very hot water if you want more coffee."

"I definitely want more coffee." Tam gathered up the mugs from the table. "Do you think I should have a retirement party?"

"Yes, of course. A big official handing-over-the-reins party. And I have a brilliant idea."

"Yeah?" She set the mugs on the counter and found Kip burrowing under her arm for a hug. She hid her face in Kip's hair as she teared up. The idea that she could have small moments like this every day was magical. Better late than never to stop being an idiot. "What's that?"

"We let Mercedes plan it, and we do everything she tells us."

"Oh my lord, woman. You are a genius."

BECAUSE I SAID SO

Published:	2019
Characters:	Kesa Sapiro, independent fashion designer
	Josie Sapiro, mathematics student and Kesa's younger sister
	Shannon Dealan, investigator, United States Marshals Service
	Paz Lopez, Shannon's ward and with appearances by Jennifer Lamont, actress, and Suzanne Mason, entrepreneur
Setting:	Los Angeles, California

Twenty-Nine, Prime Number and Good Omen

THE M-WORD

(October, 6 Years Later)

"Are you sure I can't help?"

Kesa could hear the genuine concern in Shannon's voice. Her pride in her own self-sufficiency warred with her common sense. She eyed the three dress bags and her kit to do the final fittings for her clients. "I could use an extra hand."

Shannon bounced happily. "I'll be as discreet and helpful as Josie was, I promise."

Kesa missed her sister more than she'd admit. Josie and Paz had moved to student housing at MIT where Josie was carving out a path toward a mathematics PhD. Paz had eased into an engineering job arranged by the company that had sponsored his master's program. They'd only been gone two months, and it seemed like forever until Christmas when she'd see them both again. "I'll pay you what I paid Josie."

"You don't have to." Shannon's clear brown eyes shone with mischief. "I can think of other ways to be paid."

Fighting a blush, Kesa tried to sound prim and businesslike. Neither was easy when Shannon was playful. "That's not something I can enter into my ledger."

Moments later the dress bags were on the floor and Shannon was pushing her up against the wall for a thorough, promising kiss that she wholeheartedly returned.

The world was a miracle—a fling that had ended badly, then a second chance that had finally turned out—had led to having this amazing being in her arms and life. Someone she could count on, even lean on.

"Much as I'd like to, I don't have time for this," she managed to gasp before pulling Shannon to her for another kiss.

"I know. Consider it paying down your tab." Shannon brushed Kesa's cheek with her lips. "Come on, you can't be late."

"You drive."

Kesa didn't need to add that they would arrive sooner that way. It was the truth. Shannon was more fearless in Los Angeles's epic traffic. The three dress bags swayed on the rack fitted across the back of Kesa's Forester as they left their home near Oxford Square and headed north toward Hollywood. Kesa had already consulted the map of which streets were closed for Halloween festivities, so they had a circuitous route to the hotel adjacent to the convention center where her customers were booked for the night. It was extremely convenient that both clients were going to the same A-list event at the start of their haute couture costume evening.

With Shannon driving, Kesa was able to momentarily let go of the nerves that came with final fittings. Instead, she gazed out the window for subtle signs of autumn, her favorite season. The plum trees that showered white petals in April were slowly shedding crunchy leaves onto the streets. Small neighborhood parks had the occasional maple tree that teased a hint of red.

But it wasn't daytime where the seasons really changed in Southern California. It was in the night air. Instead of wafts of citrus and warm cedar, their evenings on the patio were slowly filling with earthy aromas of mold and the crackle of drier leaves. The rippling ocean breezes had shifted to crisp air from the north. Evening tea was scented with cinnamon, cardamom, and ginger. She drank it year-round, but in autumn it felt natural and correct—enough so that Shannon would have some as well.

"Check out the zombie squad." Shannon briefly lifted one hand from the wheel to point.

Kesa leaned into the cool air blowing out of the air-conditioning vent. "Cheerleaders—good choice. They can wear shorts and tank tops. Great job on getting the dangling eyeballs to stay on." She consulted the map she'd printed out in four pieces and taped together. "Turn left at Sixth. We have to go around the Melrose Street Party."

"So Highland to Santa Monica? Or to Sunset Boulevard?"

"Not that far. Looks like Willoughby is good, and then we cross Santa Monica right before it hits the 101." Kesa consulted her phone map. "The 101 is a parking lot."

"So the longest part of our four-mile trip will be gridlocked at the stoplight."

"We love LA, don't we?" She slid her hand onto Shannon's thigh to feel the warmth of her. "Thanks for spending your afternoon with me, especially since you just got back from your business trip."

"Babe, like anything else would be more important. You know I love Halloween, and there was nothing I couldn't do from home this morning."

"Well, coming with me does mean you're not finishing the paint in the guest bedroom."

Shannon threw her a look of mock innocence. "Whyever would I be avoiding that?"

Kesa took a guess, based on how guardedly neutral Shannon's response had been when they'd painted a sample stripe on the wall. "Because you don't like the color?"

Shannon drew out *um* for several seconds.

"It's okay to tell me. It *is* brighter than I thought it would be. More hot pink than a lively azalea."

"Hot, hot pink."

"I'm maybe not as good with paint as I am fabric," she allowed.

"You're excellent with it. The sample chip was too small to get the whole impact, that's all."

"This weekend we'll pick something else."

They started and finished a mini-sode podcast from *My Favorite Murder* while they inched forward in the queue to cross Santa Monica Boulevard. The hotel parking lot was being heavily screened, but Kesa had secured the necessary vendor pass to take a four-hour space. Shannon and the Subaru easily handled the steep, tight turns up the corkscrew ramps to the spot they'd been allotted.

If Kesa knew her clients, the first one would take three hours. The second perhaps forty-five minutes. Which was one reason why Kesa adored Jennifer Lamont. She didn't waste time being a diva.

Her first appointment, though, was with mother and daughter B-list influencers, and the mother thought being a diva came with that territory. The duo was also eager to score Instagram points by wearing the same designer as bona fide, way more than Internet-famous A-lister Jennifer Lamont. #DesignsbyKesa would be making the reels and stories tonight. Tomorrow she expected to be taking calls and making appointments for party gowns for the next year. For all of that, she could put up with diva attitude.

All in all, after a couple of pandemic-fueled bad years and the setback of cancelled orders when the devastating wildfires cancelled the events they were for, she finally felt cautiously hopeful.

Shannon eased into the narrow parking space. "I'm curious—if both clients are staying at the event hotel, how do they walk the red carpet?"

"They get in a limo at the other entrance and are driven around to the red-carpet line." Kesa didn't have to see Shannon's eyes to know she had rolled them hard. "It's all about appearances."

"I know. And I'm glad it's making you a success." Shannon triggered the back hatch to open. Kesa ducked under it to set her kit on the ground.

"This season I feel like I've turned the corner. I'd have never been able to do that big bride and six bridesmaids party without hiring sewers. They remembered me from before, and it all worked out." She checked that the large tackle box she used for sewing supplies was firmly latched. Chasing thimbles and spools down the parking ramp wasn't on today's agenda. "Fingers crossed I can afford a workshop again soon. The space I was in is still empty. I just have to come up with the deposits now that I can also show my income is back to where it was before lockdown. *Finally.*"

"The very same place? It was a great fit for you."

Kesa had ugly cried the day she'd moved all her supplies out of her workshop and into storage. Her ego had been further battered by not being able to kick in for expenses and the mortgage on their new house. It didn't matter that Shannon's jump from the Marshals Service to private fraud investigation had been highly lucrative. Her income more than covered the move and higher mortgage for the larger house.

They'd spent the first few weeks of "everything will go back to normal soon" unpacking, thinking it was an unexpected vacation. For Shannon, normal had come back quickly. She worked remotely, and after vaccines had been released, she'd cautiously returned to working at the office. It had taken more than two years before Kesa's clients began to call again, and many were on shoestring budgets after equally lean years. The requests had kept her busy and salved her ego but had done little for her bank account.

At least she'd been able to use some of her free time to grocery shop for Auntie Ivy and her elderly friends in the apartment complex where they lived and played Mahjong every week. She wouldn't accept payment from them but did leave with containers of homemade Filipino dishes to share with Shannon. At least she'd felt *useful* when pandemics and wildfires made her feel so helpless.

Shannon snapped the portable garment rack upright and moved the three heavy bags onto it. "After everybody is all costumed, I heard of a new place with great bibimbap and bulgogi. Just opened on the edge of Koreatown."

"That sounds wonderful. Let's see how it goes."

They trundled toward the elevator and finally had to take one going up to the top of the parking garage to then go down to the second-floor access bridge that linked to the hotel. The Marquis Hotel and Convention Center hosted The Lights and Frights Ball every year. The red carpet began at seven; A-listers would arrive no earlier than eight.

One thing was for certain: Kesa wouldn't leave until Jennifer Lamont was one thousand percent happy. But first, the B-listers.

Finally in the hallway to their first stop, Kesa gave Shannon the brief. "You're probably not going to care much for these clients. The daughter is nice, but the mother…Don't get defensive when she's rude. It's part of what I'm getting paid big bucks for—putting up with some people's egos. They're going to promote my brand on top of writing me a big check. Maybe after I get set up and start altering you could go for a nice long coffee break?"

Shannon was already nodding. "Probably a good idea. Just because people are rich or famous doesn't mean they can be crap to other people, you know."

"I know." She smooched Shannon on the cheek. "I *promise* you will not see that behavior at the second appointment."

* * *

Kesa knew her customers, that was for sure. And knew her too. Shannon was beyond glad to get out of the hotel suite. It was *very* hard not to react to the client's imperious tone and borderline hysteria every time she checked her socials. Kesa's equanimity in the face of it was nothing short of masterful.

She made her way into the late-afternoon sun and decided more coffee wasn't going to be nearly as good as a walk in the sunshine. After four days in chilly Chicago with its gray skies, Los Angeles sunshine tingling across her nose felt great. It would help with the jet lag, too.

After picking Shannon up at the airport last night, Kesa had worked several more hours, long after Shannon had crashed.

She hadn't even had the chance to tell Kesa the big news that her firm, Integrity Investigations, was merging with a larger, even more prestigious firm. The best news was that the new company definitely wanted Shannon to stay on as it underwent a huge reorganization. Sterling Fraud Investigations was the gold standard of financial investigation and forensic auditing.

When she'd made the hard decision to leave the Marshals Service, she hadn't expected to love her new job in financial fraud investigation so much. But she did. She still got to catch bad guys—and not the run-of-the-mill criminals. She chased down the ones who stole pension accounts or deliberately ran their companies into the ground to manipulate stock values. The ones first in line for government programs and missing in action when it was time to fulfill a contract or repay funds. The ones who had profiteered medical supplies and vaccines or took money for a wall that never got built.

Especially the ones who would drive entire economies into the ground with "too big to fail" thinking, believing they would never be held accountable. They believed that because most of the time they weren't. But every once in a while they'd leave a paper trail of bad faith. It felt so good to follow that trail and wrap them up like a gift for prosecutors. It was fulfilling.

After a half-hour roundabout walk she decided on an iced latte at a local roaster. The strip mall of businesses was typical of Los Angeles—beige exterior with vibrant mom-and-pop businesses inside. As she approached she realized the business owners were hosting early trick-or-treat for toddlers. Orange and yellow pumpkins, white-sheeted ghosts, and a smattering of black-clad pirates and finery-draped princesses wobbled their way around and sometimes directly into Shannon's knees.

Cuppa JoJo was packed with kids running in and out, followed by parents moving not nearly as quickly. She secured her frothy drink and retired to a table where she could watch the parade of little people. She had no doubt it was more joyous and less pretentious than anything on the red carpet at the convention center.

"Whoa there, pardner!" She steadied a little one in cowboy gear who'd staggered into her chair. "Are you Woody from *Toy Story*?"

She got a scowl in response. "I'm not Woody. I'm JESSIE YEE-HAW!"

"Even better." She glanced up to see a frazzled woman, with the same luminous dark brown eyes as "Jessie," glancing about frantically. Shannon waved a hand and pointed.

"Stop running away from me, Carlita."

"I'm JESSIE!"

"You've had too much candy." Mom smiled thanks at Shannon. "One day a year, right?"

Complete with one heck of a sugar coma, Shannon thought. The chaos was fun, and it distracted her from the subject she wanted to broach with Kesa. It was a tough one. For a decade after her parents' deaths, Kesa had coped with poverty and the persistent threat of losing custody of her much younger sister. The pandemic had brought back all her fears of losing everything she'd worked for. It was no surprise Kesa was prickly about money. It was the M-word they never talked about.

The other M-word, marriage, had been easy. Simple ceremony, reception the next day, lots of food and music. Unfortunately, the pandemic lockdown had derailed their honeymoon plans. Their fifth anniversary was not far off, and they still hadn't had a honeymoon. Which led directly to the Money-word, because Kesa was insisting on paying for half of it.

They'd had to lean on each other all through lockdown. There was no reason to stop. The upcoming merger meant a bonus. There was enough money in Shannon's account to easily get Kesa into her workshop again. What she really wanted was for them both to stop thinking of it as "Shannon's" account.

Her phone pinged with a text from Kesa that read, *I'll be done here in about 20.*

She replied that she was on her way and began the walk back to the hotel. The boulevard was even more crowded as city workers began moving barricades to narrow and eventually close down the entire thoroughfare. It was going to be one heck of a street party. With Josie and Paz now in Massachusetts, this would actually be the first Halloween they'd spent alone, but late-night crowds weren't a scene either of them enjoyed.

At the hotel she was kept from going to the elevators by a newly erected security checkpoint. She got out her phone to text Kesa that she would have to come down to get her in. It slipped out of her hand when she was bumped aside by a tall woman in a Baby Deadpool T-shirt and faded jeans carrying two coffees. The guard was waving her through, but she turned back at Shannon's heartfelt curse word as her phone bounced across the floor.

"I'm so sorry! The coffee's burning my hands."

"And that's why I always get a protective case." Shannon snagged her phone off the floor. Straightening, she had the unusual experience of sizing up a woman taller than she was. "Are you Suzanne Mason?"

She got a stare for an answer.

"I'm Shannon Dealan. I'm with Kesa Sapiro—she's doing the fitting for Ms. Lamont."

"Shannon, as in Kesa's wife?"

She nodded.

"Nice to meet you finally. To the guard Suzanne said, "This one's with me," and Shannon happily found herself on the other side of the barricade.

At the elevators Suzanne was clearly looking for a place to set down one of the coffees.

Might as well be helpful. "Can I hold one for you?"

"That would be great. I need to swipe the room card, or I won't be able to choose our floor."

Of course they were on one of the restricted floors. Shannon took the thick paper cup in one hand. "Wow. You weren't kidding about the boiling hot coffee."

"I'm sure it's awful, but it's going to save lives. I don't know what the machine in the room is for, but what comes out looks like coffee and tastes like chicken soup."

"How vivid. And gross."

Suzanne added dryly, "We got here last night. This morning was not pretty. Room service is slammed, so I volunteered."

Shannon remembered just in time to push the right floor to rejoin Kesa. As the doors opened she gave Suzanne the coffee back. "See you in a little bit."

Suzanne nodded. "Thanks for the assist."

A moment later she texted Kesa that she was in the hall outside the room.

After a longish pause, Kesa opened the door and drew her inside. "Nearly done. Could you gather up my kits and put them on the rack?"

"Will do." Shannon was glad to hear the effusive thanks from the mother. The gowns were stunning, both appearing to be made out of autumn leaves that Kesa had laboriously hand-cut and sewn onto a close-fitting brown underdress that matched their rich brown skin color. The mother's gown was leaves of tangerine and crimson, in contrast with the daughter's gold and butterscotch.

The shy daughter appealed to Shannon for an opinion. "Is it all right?"

With complete honesty she answered, "That color is phenomenal. Once the masks and gloves are on you'll both be autumnal dryads. For real, I've never seen anything like it."

The faces of the other three women all beamed at her, especially Kesa's.

"I meant it. They looked incredible," Shannon told Kesa once they were out in the hall and pushing the dress rack along between them. "Amazing gowns."

Kesa paused for as long as it took to smooch Shannon's cheek. "Two down, one to go."

* * *

Around the two pins pressed between her lips, Kesa said to Shannon, "Hold da folphs ride thewe."

"Lucky for you I understood that."

She quickly replaced Shannon's fingers with the pins. It was the last pleat to tack into place before she began stitching everything more securely. "Really, don't make me laugh with pins in my mouth."

Kesa sat back on her haunches and surveyed her work. Jennifer Lamont had chosen to dress as the Bride of Frankenstein. Pleated satin called to mind the costuming for ancient Rome and Grecian period films from the 1930s and 1940s, with squared-off shoulders borrowed from Elsa Lanchester's iconic hospital/bridal gown in the classic movie. A stylist was already putting finishing touches on an outlandishly bouffant black wig complete with white lightning stripes on the sides. A makeup artist would arrive shortly to add faux stitches to face, chest, arms, and legs.

Jennifer gave herself an approving nod in the mirror. "This works. It's exactly what I was thinking. It's not a copy of the movie gown, but it still screams Golden Era of Hollywood. I wonder what it would have looked like in red, as you first suggested, but I think white for a bride is better."

"We'll do a Jezebel riff at some point."

"Flaming red at a stuffy black-tie event." One expressive, elegant eyebrow lifted. "I look forward to it. Thank you for this." She put her hands in the gown's hidden pockets. "Room for my phone. And I can breathe."

"Glad you like it."

Jennifer pointed at her wife. "It's supremely unfair that she gets to put on a tuxedo and a little black mask, and that's enough to claim the whole James Bond vibe. And she only has to get dressed twenty minutes ahead of time."

Suzanne Mason looked up from her phone. "While you get to wear an incredible gown. With pockets. That you just said is comfortable." She craned her head to see the shoes. "And low-heel boots?"

"A newly electrified human female is not born knowing how to work Manolos." Jennifer looked fondly down at the boots as Kesa adjusted one final pin. "These are my Scaforas, and they fit like a dream. But I swear, next year I'm going as Marlene Dietrich in her tuxedo phase with a lovely pair of men's classic Oxfords."

"My darling, if you're going to indulge in foreplay you should wait until we're alone." Suzanne blew her wife a kiss and got a husky laugh in return. "Somebody is going to see you tonight and decide that it's time for a whole new take on Frankenstein and his bride."

Jennifer tsk-tsked. "Frankenstein was the doctor. The bride was made for the monster."

Unfazed by the correction, Suzanne went on. "See? That's some weird fantasy stuff right there. The Bride needs her own story. She leaves that whole crazy scene. Names herself. Meets a nice woman. Perfects bionic prostheses because cadaver pieces are gross, and they live happily ever after."

"I'd watch that," Shannon offered, and Kesa had to agree.

The final sewing went quickly. Even with the careful pressing of the hems and seams, it wasn't even forty-five minutes before Jennifer was fully fitted and signing off on Kesa's invoice.

Kesa was elated and exhausted all at once. As they rolled the dress rack between them on the way back to the car, she considered how insane the traffic probably was. "How far is it to the bibimbap?"

"Couple miles. But we have to get back across Santa Monica. Maybe thirty minutes?"

"That's not bad. We'd have to do that anyway to get home. The traffic is going to get worse instead of better tonight." She felt almost lightheaded as the stress of the fittings was chased away by the anticipated increase in her pitiful bank balance.

After reloading the car and a perilous, tight journey down the spiral parking ramp, they emerged into a very Hollywood twilight. Cars were honking from all directions. Spotlights swept over the inky sky, eclipsing the stars and moon, while camera flashes made human stars all the brighter. Crowds of costumed partiers were streaming across the side street toward the block party. Fortunately, the Highway Patrol was controlling traffic which kept drivers from gridlocking the primary intersections. Her stomach growled loudly as they finally turned south toward Koreatown.

To her surprise, as the traffic cleared, Shannon coasted into a drugstore parking lot. "Need something?"

"No, I just—I decided I don't want to have this conversation at the restaurant."

Kesa felt a pain in her chest as if her heart had stopped beating. "What do you mean? What conversation?"

"It's okay, it's not bad." Shannon shut off the engine and turned to face her. There was enough light for Kesa to see a nervous half-smile. "At least I don't think it's bad."

"Work news?"

"Yes, in fact, Integrity is merging with Sterling, like we all thought we would when the boss retires. I'm slated to get a promotion to a forensic team manager, and they're handing out bonuses."

"Do we have to move?"

For some reason Shannon's smile was a little wobbly. "No. We stay right here."

"That's all good news then, right? Why do you look like there's bad news now?"

"Not bad. It's just—" She took a deep breath. "I want to talk about money. As in *our* money."

Had she spent too much on groceries? Was it her one indulgence in upscale coffee? "I'll have a big deposit at the bank tomorrow. Lamont's accountant always pays promptly, too."

"I'm really happy for you, that it worked out. That's not what I'm talking about. The thing is, I love my job, I'm getting a raise and a bonus, and I really want you to have your workshop back."

"I want that too."

"Then what are you waiting for?"

"I don't have the money." She realized where Shannon was headed. "I don't want to take yours."

"It's not mine, Key. It's *ours*."

"It doesn't feel that way to me."

Shannon bit her lower lip. "I wish it did. We, us together, can afford to front your business, the same way we, us together, can pay the mortgage on *our* house. And go on a honeymoon, finally."

Kesa did her best to quell the tight, uncomfortable pressure in her chest. "But you've been paying for almost everything all along."

"Right now. There'll come a time when maybe the table will turn. It's a chance I'm willing to take because we're in it together. If you won't let me have your back, would you have mine if I needed it?"

"It's totally different."

"How?"

Kesa didn't know what to say. She'd been struggling for so long she didn't know how it would feel if life got easier. Wouldn't she always feel like she was borrowing from Shannon? She hated being in debt. Having to declare bankruptcy after her parents' death had made sure of that.

"If you can't say how, is there anything I've been doing to make you feel like I resent our current financial realities?"

"No, it's not you. It's me. I know that Josie and Paz share everything. Maybe it's easier to do when neither of them has a lot more."

"I get that it's imbalanced, but it won't always be. And so what if it is? Did you marry me for my paycheck?"

"No…That you had one did count in your favor. I'm the one whose money went up in smoke."

"Not your doing. We got by better than most. Safer than most. There's no reason you can't check out the workspace and get it back. We can afford it."

"You mean now that you have the new job and a bonus?"

"Actually?" Shannon's swallow was loud. "We've been able to afford it all along."

"So why are you bringing this up now?" She worried at a tiny crack in her thumbnail.

"Because I was scared to."

That made her look up. "I'm scary?"

"Money is a tough subject, especially for you after what you've been through most of your life. You're intense when you're focused, but you're not scary." At that Shannon truly smiled. "Except when you *mean* to be scary, and I like it. Maybe later?"

The fact that Shannon sounded a little flustered at the thought made Kesa grin in the dark. She brushed a fingertip across the back of Shannon's hand. "Are you saying you'd like me to insist on a trick or two before lots of treats?"

Shannon made a satisfying growling sort of sound. "I'm not sure what that might mean, but I like the possibilities."

She leaned across the seat to rub her cheek on Shannon's shoulder and breathe her in. *This is all good*, she told herself. "Can we have dinner? I need to think."

They were parked outside the restaurant before Kesa broke the silence. "I think—I get what you're saying. At my age and after all my hard work, doing anything because of my parents is silly. I don't want to be pigheaded for reasons I can't even put into words."

"I too prefer to have reasons when I'm pigheaded."

She swatted Shannon's arm. "You know what I mean. Can you show me on paper how we can afford it? Like the way we worked out we could afford the house, before the world went to hell?"

Shannon squeezed her hand. "We should always do that about the big decisions. You shouldn't take my word for it. And maybe there are costs I don't know about. I'm pretty good with a spreadsheet, you know."

"You are a genius with a spreadsheet. Especially when you do that thing with the colors where good decision is bright, pretty lime green and bad decision is a murky, fetid red." She twisted her wedding ring around on her finger, loving as always the *sapiro* chips inset into the gold. Shannon had said the sapphires were like her eyes. Her parents' marriage had been a mess of lies, debt, and neglect. *I'm not going to let them take anything else from me.* "Okay then."

Shannon took a sharp breath, as if surprised. "Really?"

"Yes, and I'd like to have our honeymoon finally."

"So would I. And I would like to have a bibimbap bowl."

Kesa laughed and got out of the car. The night air was pungent with garlic and ginger. "You're in luck. We're parked right in front of a place that serves them, and I smell so many delicious things right now."

At the door, Kesa paused long enough to pull Shannon down to her to kiss her softly on the lips. "I adore you."

"That's good, because I'm crazy about you. From that very first moment."

Kesa reluctantly let go. "The food smells so good I'm going to faint."

"I can't have that." Shannon held the door for Kesa. "Not when I am looking forward to the tricks and treats."

CAR POOL

Published:	1993
Characters:	Anthea Rossignole, cost accountant
	Shay Sumoto, environmental engineer
	Adrian and Harold, gay male friends and coworkers
Setting:	Oakland and San Jose, California

The fourth is for freedom.

Previous *Frosting on the Cake* stories:
    "Mechanics" in *Frosting 1*.
    "Divided Highway" in *Frosting 2*,
    which introduces Anthea and Harold's son,
    Henry.

The title of this story was inspired by "Perhaps the World Ends Here" from *The Woman Who Fell From the Sky* by Poet Laureate and musician Joy Harjo.

THE WORLD HEALS AT THE KITCHEN TABLE

(November, 32 Years Later)

"How do they not break their bones? Or smash their heads in?" Anthea huddled closer to Adrian, wishing she'd brought a blanket to protect her backside from the hard metal bleacher.

Adrian waved his hands at the field of combat. "I don't know."

In front of them, the combatants lined up across the line of scrimmage, seven versus seven. Puffs of breath hung between them in the chilly air. They were all yelling, and Anthea had no idea how any of them knew when a play started or ended. No one had remembered to bring a whistle and there was no referee anyway. Adrian had tried that just once and never again.

For no reason Anthea could figure out, Shay ran hard for about ten yards, then turned to wave her arms. She was smaller by nearly a foot than the shortest other player, and she always seemed to get free to catch the ball if thrown to her. This time, Harold faked a throw to her, then shoveled the ball to his son,

Henry, who tucked it in and spun his light-footed way through the sea of hands reaching for the flag on his belt.

Finally tripped up, he slid face-first through the puddles that gave the annual contest at the local school's grassy field its name: The Mud Bowl.

Harold likewise got tripped and went down with a sloshing splash. Anthea felt Adrian flinch at the loud *oooooof*. Then he laughed at the follow-up expletive.

Anthea yelled, "You're getting too old for this!"

"Hey!" Shay put her hands on her hips. She remained the only player not bathed in mud. Her shoes were soaked, though.

"I was talking to the Old Man out there."

"Hey!" Harold was likewise offended. "Who are *you* calling old?"

"You're all old," Henry announced, to the cheers and agreements of the cousins in their teens and twenties.

"Be careful, my young Padawan." Harold flexed his broad, sturdy shoulders. "Age and treachery will always overcome youth and enthusiasm."

A few moments later another play ensued, more mud splashed, and Shay caught the ball but lost her flag.

"Mama is going to hose them all off," Anthea said to Adrian. "I legit cannot tell where the mud stops, and Henry's face begins."

"And all three of them will get head colds."

"And we'll feed them turkey soup and stuffing waffles and say 'poor baby' like we do every year. Though I don't think Henry gets much TLC from his housemates."

"Don't be too sure there's no TLC. Harold thinks he has a girlfriend. A theyfriend, I should say. Harold isn't sure of anything except that a long-haired person seems to be coming to the games to cheer him on as well. He's trying to be Mr. Cool Dad and not intrude." He winced as Harold decided to end a play by sliding across a mud pond on one hip.

"Seriously? I'd be Not Cool Mom introducing myself. Like I'd bring cookies and completely chat them up." Anthea tried not to pout that this was the first she was hearing about her son's possible romantic relationship. But then again, proud dad Harold went down to Santa Cruz to watch Henry play rugby during his last eligible season as an undergrad. "How is it we don't know anything for sure?"

Adrian waved a long, bony hand at the field. "Feed the child, see the child through life-threatening illness, teach the child, and if you do it all well, the child lives their own life away from you as the final reward."

"True that. We all wanted him to be safe, and happy, and independent, and then we got what we wanted, and it's not quite what we wanted."

"Look at that smile. Just like his father's the day we met."

Anthea remembered. Harold and Adrian had found their romantic pathway much smoother than Anthea and Shay had. "I think there's more of Harold in him than me."

"Well, yes, the skin. The hair, those eyes. But he's got your hands." He broke off as Henry bobbled the ball and ended up dropping it. "If he had his father's, he would have caught that. And he bakes like you do. Did you see Mama's reaction to the apple cake he brought?"

"I did. She was button-popping proud. The powdered sugar leaves on top are very pretty." Anthea was kind of button-popping proud too.

That Harold's mother invited them to the Johnson family Thanksgiving every year was nothing short of a miracle. When she'd finally reached out to her son, after a long estrangement caused by her deep homophobia, she'd never apologized but had instead said that God challenged her to leave judgment to him. She and Harold had found a bridge for communication because Henry—Mama Johnson's only grandchild—existed. Harold and Henry had also both made positive connections with wider family scattered all over northern California.

Adrian gestured at the thermos of coffee on the bench in front of them. "Do you want more?"

"No. Oh, I nearly forgot. Next month University Theater is showing all three original *Lord of the Rings* movies, extended cut in a fifteen-hour marathon. Wanna?"

"Why do you have to ask? Yes, of course, count on both of us, though Harold might not be free."

"Shay says it's after their consulting schedule eases up for the season, so it should be clear for him too." Anthea tucked her hands inside her coat sleeves. She ought to have remembered that nothing was colder than a foggy fifty-degree day in the East Bay. The breeze seemed to come from all directions and went straight down the back of her coat. "I adore being retired."

"Me too. Now we have to convince the people we're married to that it's time to scale back and we can really party."

"Shay says next year they'll go to half time. So many young people are entering the environmental science field that it feels like they have great options for mentorees."

"Meanwhile, our tax season cometh. Training starts second week of January."

"As usual? You're going to site manage again?"

"I know it makes me crazy, but it's worth it."

"You're good at it." Anthea was speaking the absolute truth. From January to April Adrian was the king of Volunteer Tax Preparation in the Oakland area for seniors and low-income people. He recruited tax preparers to fill the desks, made sure the computers had power, created the triage for the appointments line, and farmed out the work so nobody got all the easy ones or all the exceptions. As if that wasn't enough, he'd approached the local CPA firms for volunteers to spend just one day helping out during the final, hectic week.

Anthea put her accounting skills to use for the whole tax season, volunteering two long days every week and all the Saturdays for the final four weeks the program was open. She'd been paid well all her life to do accounting for corporations. Working for free to help someone who really needed every penny of a small refund—it was likely one of the most rewarding things she'd ever done. Their entire East Bay region had filed for more than thirty million dollars in refunds on behalf of their clients.

She felt a little guilty that it was so easy for her to do something so directly good. But there were also bad days when someone working three jobs had been under-withheld by all of them and owed half a month's rent. "It's good while it lasts and good when it's over."

"Speaking of over—I think the game is? Maybe?" Adrian tucked the coffee flask into his backpack.

Shay was as yet unmuddied and successfully fending off hugs and high fives expressly designed to make her so. "I have earned a plateful of food," she announced when she reached the bleachers. "And seconds of corn casserole."

Anthea smooched her. "Yes, you have. You played very well."

Shay's sneakers squelched with every step. "You say that because I'm not covered in muck."

"That's my rulebook, yes."

The mire-dripping participants continued to throw the ball back and forth and trash-talk as they all walked the narrow street back to the hundred-year-old bungalow where Harold had grown up. Anthea had offered to stay and help, but there were already so many aunties making sure everything was ready that it had seemed prudent to get out of the way.

By the time she, Shay, and Adrian turned the final corner they could hear the shouts and protests as Harold's oldest uncle turned on the garden hose and sprayed them all from the safety of the porch.

Mama appeared at the end of the driveway with a stack of towels. "Nobody is tracking mud onto my clean floors. Come get dried off."

Shay made a detour to the car to change out her squelching sneakers for respectable socks and loafers. Henry was already rinsed and at the side door where he was busy shucking off his shirt as he shivered.

"Go into the utility room and finish changing, and put your clothes in the washer," Mama ordered, as she had every year the Mud Bowl was played.

"Thanks, Nana." Henry gave his grandmother a damp kiss on the cheek and did as he was told.

Anthea, for her part, was transfixed in the breezeway as fresh sage and thyme tickled at her nose, followed by the tang of cranberry and smoke of bitter greens. The mingled smell of celery and onion with butter and roasting turkey sent her stomach into an ache of anticipation. "The house smells so good!"

"The potatoes just came to a boil, and the turkey will be out in about fifteen minutes." Mama continued handing out towels. "We eat in forty-five, after the gravy's made."

"Put me to work," Anthea told Mama. "I can mash potatoes with the best of them."

"I was hoping you'd do it. That trick of warming the cream before you add it makes them so fluffy."

Adrian lingered to help Harold and Henry get changed, while Anthea slithered through the crowded kitchen and into the living room to see if there was anything she could help with while the potatoes cooked.

The room was usually orderly. Dark-green and navy-blue area rugs were squared precisely under furniture centered under the overhead chandelier. The plastic-sheathed, high-back sofa and wide, padded chairs had been pushed to the walls to make room for folding tables, card tables, assorted chairs, a piano bench, and a knee-high table for the toddlers who were currently being amused by the young cousin Anthea thought was working on her teaching certificate. Her reading aloud of *The Monster at the End of the Book* was drawing shouts of laughter from the small people.

The first time Anthea had visited the house had been cold and Mrs. Johnson an angry woman, bitterly getting by in a world she saw as only hostile. Though Anthea would never be thankful for Henry's illness, it was the possibility of losing Henry that had melted Mama. She now moved like a woman years younger. Anthea had felt as if she'd were witnessing a miracle the day Mama had laughed for joy to see her son in the doorway with healthy, recovering Henry on his hip.

Now the house was a human rainbow of movement as tablecloths and plates and napkins and water glasses were put in place. The sideboard was a mass of slow cookers. Anthea sniffed with delight over each one, smelling mac and cheese, corn and jalapeño casserole, and maple-bourbon sweet potatoes. Side by side were two empty cookers, both set to low and preheating—one for her mashed potatoes and the other for the gravy. Boxes on the sofa and chairs protected Henry's apple cake, for one, plus Anthea's platter of yellow butter cupcakes filled with chocolate mousse. There were also mounds of gingersnaps and two each of pumpkin, apple, and pecan pies brought by the rest of the family.

Anthea gently straightened an art print of a Harriet Powers quilt from the late 1800s that had been knocked off-kilter in the melee. She noticed that the quilt rack with Mama's mother's beautiful work had been moved somewhere to safety.

Mama paused in her continual movement between kitchen and dining areas. "Now what are we forgetting?"

"I can't think of a thing." Shay rejoined them looking dapper and dry.

Anthea gestured at the sofa's dessert boxes. "I'm figuring there's two slices of pie for each person and then some."

"The Good Lord knows the young people will eat their share and ours too if we let them." Mama tweaked a corner of a tablecloth before bustling away.

The slightly ajar front door opened farther, and a shy-faced young man holding a bag of sweet dinner rolls poked his head in. Anthea had the impression that he was about to back out. She understood—the chaos was not for the faint of heart.

Shay greeted him with, "Are you looking for Mrs. Johnson's house?"

"Yes, I, uh, this is the right place?"

"Sure is."

His soft, Southern accent made everything a question. "I'm Neeshi? My papa's brother worked with her at the hospital for a long time before he retired back to Alabama. And when I said I was moving here, he said to look her up, and I did, and she invited me to supper?"

Shay shook his hand. "Of course she did. I'm Shay. Let me get her out of the kitchen."

"Welcome." Anthea drew him into the house and closed the door. "I'm Anthea. That was my wife, Shay, and I'm the mother of Mrs. Johnson's grandson, Henry. You do not have to remember all the names. At least not yet."

"That was your wife?"

Anthea's quick glance took in an anxious expression that eased away as she nodded. "Yes, long time now." Thinking she was on the right track, she added, "Harold, Mrs. Johnson's son, is here somewhere with his husband, Adrian."

"That's terrific." Neeshi's nervousness dissipated.

"Is this Neeshi Williams?" Mama made her way through the maze of tables and chairs to give Neeshi an enveloping, slightly floury embrace. "I'm so glad you could join us. You look just like your uncle."

"I hope I do." Neeshi glanced at the front door. "I need to step out for a minute? My friend drove me here and I wasn't sure this was the right house so he's waiting for me to wave."

"He's going to his family?"

"No, Mrs. Johnson. His family didn't ask him."

All in a flash, Anthea could see the regret in Mama's eyes for the almost decade that she hadn't spoken to her only child. "Well, you go tell him to park that car and join us. I won't hear otherwise."

The young man's face blossomed into a wide, pleased smile, and he hurried out.

"He seems so sweet," Anthea observed.

"He does, and everybody should be with family…" After a pause, Mama's voice steadied. "With family today."

"My parents didn't do this," Anthea shared. "We lived in a beige house with gray tile, and we went to the country club for every holiday."

"That sounds lonely."

"It was. Finding Shay changed everything for me. I went from getting through the day to actually having a life and a family."

Mama didn't say anything, but she briefly squeezed Anthea's arm.

Neeshi and his friend, shoulders bumping, came up the front steps.

"Thank you, Mama," Anthea said. "There's a poem that says the world heals at the kitchen table. Or is it 'thrives'? Either way, I think it's true."

"When you know better, do better. That's a favorite of mine." She stepped forward to meet the newcomer and assure him that there was plenty of food. "You come right in. We'll find you a chair."

PAPERBACK ROMANCE

Published: 1992
Characters: Carolyn Vincense, romance novelist
                Alison McNamara, Carolyn's agent
                Nicola Frost, symphony conductor
Setting: Hot spots of Europe and Sacramento, California

The third is for turning on.

Previous *Frosting on the Cake* stories:
        "Key of Sea" in *Frosting 1*.
        "Payout" in *Frosting 2*.

MERELY PLAYERS

(December, 33 Years Later)

Ho bloody ho ho.
Nicola Frost frowned at her reflection, displeased with the gray at her temples, the lines around her mouth, and—most of all—the boredom in her eyes.
Do a favor for someone, and this is what you get. Instead of Cannes or Majorca, or any place warm and sipping blue umbrella drinks with Patricia, she was alone in a dreary and cold part of California that had nowhere near the gaiety of San Francisco or the glitter of Hollywood.
Sacramento. The capital of the huge, diverse state.
The concertmaster who'd greeted her at the airport had cheerfully explained how so many more interesting places were only a few hours away. If only Nick was here for more than a week, or stayed a few days after the gala concert, or could drive on the wrong side of the bloody road, she could see Lake Tahoe or Napa Valley or the wild, rocky surf and bluffs of Mendocino. The towering natural landmarks of Yosemite.

Patricia was the ambidextrous driver, and Patricia had planted herself at her cottage in Surrey for the duration of the holidays.

It hardly helped that the favor she'd agreed to was for her first love. In spite of having loved again and better since, Carolyn still occupied a place inside her that couldn't belong to anyone else.

Nick was old enough to understand how flexible the human heart could be in matters of love. She loved Patricia and welcomed Patricia's love. Over the past couple of decades, they'd run the gamut of deliriously passionate to cup-of-tea content and everything in between. Patricia had that someone in her past too, that someone to whom she always said, "How can I help?" and "Of course I will," because affection like that got more precious with every passing year.

Especially after the last hellish ones. The Sacramento Community Symphony wasn't the only orchestra that had lost personnel to the pandemic. Like many other arts organizations, SCS found themselves mired in debt from performing and rehearsal halls they owned but couldn't use for nearly three years. There simply wasn't enough profit from the usual offerings to vanquish the debt. They'd managed to scrimp through their last season by borrowing a music director from a university.

"Of course I will," she'd said when Carolyn had asked. The sun had been shining six months ago. And of course she would.

But she didn't have to like it.

Even with the white streaks at her temples, her short black hair still looked good spiky, so she left it that way for the afternoon of video calls ahead of her. At least she would get to talk to Patricia over lunch. After that, she and the SCS concertmaster would shore up numerous live rehearsal details that would pull together all the pieces of remote practice over the next two days. The woman was enthusiastic and overflowing with determination to make the week of holiday concerts the most successful in the symphony's history. How could it be anything less with a world-class conductor at its helm?

Subscriber tickets were sold out, and general admission tickets went on sale tomorrow and were certain to sell out as well.

Her watch pinged a reminder for lunch. After a quick visit to the kitchen in the condominium apartment the Friends of the Sacramento Community Symphony had provided for her, she carried a peanut butter and sweet pickle sandwich to the work desk where her laptop screen was slowly changing colors. She hadn't admitted to Patricia that one of her guilty pleasures while traveling in the US was peanut butter. Compared to the rest of the world, Americans were insane for the stuff. She found it weirdly and satisfyingly addictive in all its many forms.

Patricia's smiling face, framed by her tousled blond hair, was a welcome sight. Her blue eyes were relaxed as she toasted Nick with a glass of red wine. "Too early for you?"

"Nothing but meetings all afternoon, so yes."

Patricia held up her plate of crackers, cheese, and orange slices so Nick could see it. "What are you eating?"

Nick tilted her plate at the laptop camera. "A sandwich."

"Are there vegetables?"

"Cucumber."

Patricia rolled her eyes. "You mean pickles."

"It's whole wheat bread and vegetarian. Ergo, health food."

"You look tired. Didn't you sleep after you got in last night?"

"I did. I've been regretting this decision and it's making me cross." She had a bite of her sandwich. It was as good as she'd expected—at least there was that.

"Is it really going to be that bad?"

"No. The symphony and the hall are perfectly adequate."

"Ouch." Patricia chased a bite of water cracker and what looked like smoked Gouda with a swallow of red wine. "*Adequate* is not a review you've ever yearned for."

"They aspire to please their audience."

"You say that like it's a bad thing."

"It's not," she said irritably. "But it is. There's nothing in this concert to lift anyone out of themselves. It's a *Pops* concert—candy floss for the ears."

"That sounds so elitist. It must be something Oscar opined."

She smiled at the recollection of her early mentor. "It likely was. And of course it was elitist. He was elitist. I'm elitist."

"This is true."

They ate in silence for a minute, but Nick knew from Patricia's pensive expression that she had an observation that Nick was probably not going to care for. "Say what you're thinking."

"Couple of things. I mean, I get it. A Holiday Pops concert at a second-tier symphony is not your usual oeuvre. But it's still music. It's still going to make people *feel*. That's the point of art, isn't it?"

"No, that's—"

"Okay, it's not the *only* point of art. Yesterday at the Ockley book fair—"

"Oh yes, how was your signing?"

Patricia grinned. "Adequate. Spectacularly adequate."

"Excellent. Do go on, though. I interrupted your thought." Nick realized she did want to hear Patricia out.

"Anyway, afterward I went for a walk through the local Christmas Market. They hold it in the sculpture garden and green. I wish you could have been there, it was sweet and simple and just what I needed. Oh!" Her eyes lit up. "I got a ripping good small-batch cherry cordial, and a sinus-clearing Stilton, and an enormous molasses-ginger biscuit."

"Sounds delightful. When I got in last night there was a gift basket waiting, and the Napa Valley soft cheese with a streak of sharp blue running through it would have made you cry."

"Are you going to bring me some?"

"I'll share as much of the cheese as you will of the biscuit."

She narrowed her eyes. "Fine. I ate the whole thing on the train ride home."

Nick grinned. "There's exactly nothing left of the cheese. I ran out of crackers and finished it with a spoon," she admitted without a hint of shame.

"You are a cretin, Nicola Frost, and I love you."

"I love that you love me."

She laughed outright and blew Nick a kiss. "Anyway, of course there was music. A local group playing carols. The penny whistle player was quite all right, and there were two fiddlers and one of those portable keyboards you blow into. What's that called?"

"A melodica."

"One of those. It was jolly and bright, and children were dancing. And I thought there were two stories possible about the group."

Nick relaxed, long familiar with Patricia's compulsion to create stories about nearly everything she saw. "Tell me."

"On the one hand, frustrated musicians who fell so far from success they were reduced to playing at a fair. On the other, fulfilled musicians who, year after year, knew they would make children dance and the adults keep time. Who know that the people they lived near and around admired them and looked to them for that joy. And I thought of that question you ask your students."

"You're going to quote me to me?"

"Darling, put your eyebrow back down. Why would I quote you when you know the question I mean."

She delayed answering by taking a very large bite of her sandwich. There was so much peanut butter she had to fetch a glass of water. Patricia ate her orange slices one by one with the air of someone who has solved life's great mysteries and it was up to Nick to admit it.

Mouth finally unglued, Nick gave Patricia the side-eye she deserved. "The question I ask is 'What are you going to give back to the world with your precious talent?' You're saying that a tune you can dance to is enough?"

"If that's the limit of what you can give, isn't that the definition of giving your all?"

Nick closed her eyes to better hear her thoughts. "I know that it's not for me to judge if anyone but me is doing all they can—or even should—with the talent they have. I also know that during these concerts *I* could be doing more but the players, some of them, can't follow me there." She opened her eyes again to judge Patricia's reaction.

The soft blue gaze was filled with patience, and yes, lingering smugness. "You got them to refine the list. Instead of only secular and Christian there's a Jewish folk melody and a devotional raga, aren't there? And you will enjoy the infinite canon from Senegal, you always do."

Aware that she was being petulant, but liking Patricia's attempts to cheer her up, Nick said, "There's still a 'Frosty the Snowman' medley and sing-along."

"There is better and worse Beethoven. Better and worse Bach. It's all music, and music is the language we all speak."

"That's rude," Nick retorted. "First you make me quote myself and now you're quoting Bernstein at me."

Patricia blinked with complete innocence. "Was it Bernstein? I thought I was quoting you."

She was entirely too smug. "Even more rude."

"Are you meeting up with Carolyn and Alison tonight?"

"After the big donor meet and greet. I'll see them there and then we're going to a speakeasy. Which might be what they call their house—I'm unclear on that part."

"Sounds delightful—and far better than *adequate*."

She felt her petulance fade and gave Patricia a grateful smile. "I do love you, you know. Tell me more about the book fair."

* * *

Meet and greets with arts donors were the same the world over. Caviar on canapés, sparkling wine in plastic flutes, and air thick with perfume. She spotted Alison McNamara, Carolyn's wife, early on. As usual, Alison was sharply turned out in a tailored black business suit and brilliant-hued blouse—emerald tonight—and nevertheless managed to look a bit disheveled, but in a way that conveyed she cared more about talking to you than she did about her hair. Patricia had that kind of artless charm, and Nick understood how Carolyn was captivated by it.

Alison was also irreverent and kind, and Nick had long let go of jealousy at the woman's good fortune to be with Carolyn. Instead she was genuinely happy to know how deeply and clearly Carolyn loved and was loved. Which, she realized, made her also aware of her own good fortune to have also found someone who fit her so splendidly.

Alison broke off her conversation and made a beeline for Nick. This was appreciated because Alison's impetuous hug effectively ended a tedious, one-sided discussion of What Was Wrong with Music Today with an older man who hadn't listened to any music created in this century or the one before it.

After the usual inquiries about the flight, and if she liked her accommodations, Alison said, "Did all that pandemic downtime turn into the memoir we talked about—was it in Vienna? Six years ago?"

Alison was also a very good literary agent, with her wife as her favorite client. "Carly Vincent" had a bookshelf full of admired and successful romance and intrigue novels. Nick had read the series about the symphony conductor who sometimes took spy jobs from Interpol with amused and self-conscious delight.

"Vienna, I think you're right." She shrugged. "I made notes. I wondered, a lot, about hiring a professional writer to help me. I asked Patricia if she wanted to help me, and she said no, we'd kill each other, and she's likely right. She's as touchy about her novels as I am my music."

"All you arty types are touchy. You can be nice people and you're interesting, but you're *all* touchy."

"Since I work with a great many arty types, I can't disagree with you."

Nick recognized in Alison's expression the slight distancing that occurred when she consulted the part of her brain that was devoted entirely to the intricate relationships of the publishing world. "If you brought it to market in the next two years, your timing would be good. I'm seeing strong interest in rights auctions for memoir and biography rights. And—sorry to say, really—I think there's a lot of people who have no idea you spent your first few years as a conductor letting the world think you were a man. People would eat that story up, and there's a vast dialog about gender and presentation that you could speak to from a historic perspective—sorry again, but none of us are exactly young anymore. You were audacious, young, talented, and not going to let the classical world sideline you, down with the patriarchal limits on gender roles—"

"That's giving me a lot of credit when all I wanted was to conduct."

"Did you have to want more? You changed the world anyway, because you believed you should have a chance to reach your full potential."

Alison's reaction was one of the reasons Nick had never fully embraced the idea of a memoir. People wanted to give her more credit than she felt she was due. It had been a reckless gambit and not even her idea. Oscar had suggested she register for a contest audition a second time, in a man's suit, sans jewelry and makeup. Her height alone, combined with an already angular face and large hands, would let the male judges see what they expected to see. And they had. Neither she nor Oscar had expected the charade to become her life, just as they hadn't expected "Nicolas" Frost's meteoric rise through the ranks of classical conductors.

"People would welcome a true story about how talent isn't enough," Alison was saying. "It takes risk and luck. And isn't it a fact that since symphonies began using blind auditions women are represented something like thirty percent more in top-tier orchestras?"

Nick acknowledged the truth of it with a nod.

Alison snagged a canapé from a passing tray. "Is there still gatekeeping regarding who can get into the auditions?"

"The real gatekeeping is who can afford a quality musical training at a young age. Or any musical training at all."

"Well, yeah." Alison made a face at the cracker she'd grabbed, shrugged, and popped the whole thing into her mouth. After a swallow she went on, "That's kind of tasty. Anyway, quality musical training at a young age isn't cheap. Would that be why you sponsor not just a university chair, but also in-school music demonstrations by working musicians?"

"I pay cab fare and the like. Other people do all the work."

"It's called paying it forward. In your case, *playing* it forward."

Nick lifted an eyebrow at the horrible pun. "Because I can. I rode male privilege to the top—how could I not give as much as possible back to women? I can't ignore that my parents were able to hire me a music tutor when I was six."

"If you haven't noticed it, we are overrun with people who think they made their billions all by their own little selves and all they owe the world back is sending themselves into space."

She lifted one shoulder. "You have me there."

Alison's agent face was suddenly front and center. "It will be a great project. Thank you!"

Nick blinked. She was glad of Alison's expertise but had not intended for Alison to think Nick was pitching a project to her. When Alison fluttered her eyelashes for good measure, Nick realized it was put on. "For an agent who handles nonfiction, you mean."

"Yes, you need one of those. I know someone. She's in Paris, says what she thinks, and knows the ropes of putting something like this up for wide auction. Would you like me to call her and open up a direct line?"

"Yes, thank you. And thank you for your observations."

"What are you two whispering about?" Approaching from behind Nick, Carolyn paused to kiss Nick on the cheek before slipping her hand under Alison's arm.

She was, as always, a treat for the eyes. Her hair had gone more white than blond, and all the dear lines of her face were from laughter. Her eyes, too, had lightened over the decades, and in the shimmering party lights they were a translucent blue.

"We were talking about books, of course." Alison snagged Carolyn a canapé from a passing tray. "For you, my love."

"Perfect." Carolyn mimed a kiss at Alison before popping the sliver of toast and caviar into her mouth.

Looking at Carolyn, Nick had the same feeling as when she made an almost annual pilgrimage to Brighton Beach where her mother had taken her as a child. It was a "Good, it's still there, all's right with the world now" sense of satisfaction and security. "I was about to mention that Patricia and I are dreaming of spending a week or two in southern Spain in the spring. You're both turning sixty, and that should be celebrated."

"I'm in," Alison said quickly. "Patricia always knows where the best cheese is."

"It's one of her most admirable qualities." Nick was not joking.

"Let's make plans at the speakeasy later, shall we?" Carolyn smiled widely as she lowered her voice. "Our top donor is approaching, on my right. Nikki Crocker. You'll like her. She's a pistol."

"I will mingle." She nodded and turned to greet the newcomer.

* * *

The "speakeasy" that Carolyn had alluded to was indeed the comfortable den in their house. Nick had been delighted because it meant ham sandwiches, genuine American potato salad, and utter relaxation with two dear friends accompanied by a glass of the tawny port that Alison always had on hand. One glass had put her to sleep, but only for a minute.

Carolyn had shaken her awake. "You're jet-lagged. Let me drive you back to your digs."

"This is a first," Nick observed as she buckled herself into the passenger seat of a sporty-sized sedan. It felt all wrong to be to the right of the driver. "Alison always drives."

"She's a bad passenger, so I let her do it. But I do know how."

She did indeed. Being the passenger meant Nick had time to notice the holiday lights that the entire street had put up. Simple and yet so jolly, like the Christmas Market Patricia had described. Lots of people doing little things in harmony. God only knew the world needed more of that.

Some of the charm disappeared as Carolyn accelerated onto one of America's wide concrete highways enlivened only by billboards.

"I just remembered what I wanted to ask you about." Carolyn tapped her brakes to yield her right of way to a small black sports car darting in and out of traffic. "You mentioned in an email that you'd had a brain scan for research. Tell me all about it."

Long familiar with Carolyn's widely eclectic areas of interest and the way they folded into her novels, Nick was happy to explain. "The researchers were attempting to capture brain activity when various people were performing at what they considered their peak. As they explained it, they wanted to know what was going on in our brains when we perceive we are in mind-brain-spirit harmony."

"So you were wearing sensor things on your head while you conducted?"

"They itched and then I forgot they were there," she remembered. "I had them on while conducting and while lecturing on Span of Attention. Apparently when I talk about large orchestra setups and cueing all the moving pieces during something like Beethoven's *Ninth*, I get much the same brain activity as when I'm actually conducting it."

"That is hecka cool. So talking about it is as good as doing it?"

Nick was grateful that Carolyn was sorting out the myriad of merging lanes and weaving concrete overpasses. Finally, after turning what felt like a complete circle and half back again, the signs read "Old Town" and traffic noticeably thinned. "There's some caveats. A person likely needs to have reached that harmony repeatedly before recalling it is similar to reliving it. You've written several characters coping with PTSD, haven't you?"

"Yes, and I find all the research about it really interesting."

"These researchers began their inquiry by working backward for treatments for trauma."

"Wow."

Nick grinned to herself. "I knew you'd be intrigued by that."

"So if treating trauma is helping a person recall something bad *without* reliving it, they're researching the other direction. A regular practice of reliving moments of joy to alleviate emotional depression? That sounds like something spiritualists have been telling humankind since forever."

"Doesn't it?"

"Did you learn anything from the exercise, for yourself?"

"Though I think I knew it, I learned that, because I have reached that joyful state often enough in my life, I undoubtedly have the power to elevate my own mood."

Carolyn briefly touched her sleeve. "I remember, years ago, when you hit a lull, and you were pretty despondent about it."

Remembering too, Nick cleared her throat. "After Oscar died. I still have bouts of it." Just this morning, she might have added.

"I hope some old-fashioned holiday music and a strong sense of community will make Saturday night that powerful for you. Another moment of joy to relive."

Nick blinked. Good lord, she thought, is *that* what I'm balking at? Was she afraid that the music, the venue, or the musicians would prevent her from that ineffable state she hoped for in every performance?

And if they don't, whose fault is that?

From the past she heard Oscar say in his driest John Gielgud tone, "If you believe you can, perhaps you can. If you believe you can't, then you can't."

"Nick? Where'd you go?"

She realized that Carolyn had pulled into the condominium drop-off zone.

"Philosophical argument."

"Chicken or egg kind of thing?"

"Is it the music, the performance, or the collective energy?"

"Do you have to choose?"

She glanced at Carolyn's face illuminated by the dashboard lights. That smile was still capable of stealing a little of Nick's breath. She had that sense again, of all being right with the world because Carolyn had built a life for herself filled with love and the passion for living.

So, Nick thought, *have I.* When it's all over, did anything else matter?

She kissed Carolyn's cheek. "Thanks for the lift and the conversation."

"I might not be able to make it to that cocktail thing tomorrow, but I'll definitely see you Saturday night at the gala."

"I'm looking forward to it."

To her surprise, she was.

* * *

Saturday night Carolyn arrived at her seat to find her sister-in-law Margot clearly relieved to see her. Her brother Curt waved a greeting as he leaned over the railing to watch the musicians tune.

"Where's Ally?"

"Waiting on the valet. We allowed thirty minutes for traffic and we're still late." The symphony choir, cheerful and merry in robes of red, green, blue, and white, was already on the risers at the rear of the orchestra. The stage was arranged with the usual strings and wind instrument groupings, but there was also room carved out for a gleaming grand piano, a sitar, an assortment of hand drums, and long, hanging tubular bells.

Margot gave her an admiring look. "Is that dress new? It looks great on you."

"Thank you. It's been in mothballs for a while, but the wide collars are retro chic I'm told." Carolyn put her emerald-green velvet sleeve next to Margot's holly-red lace. "I hoped you'd be wearing your holiday finery because we totally go together."

"Is Ally wearing her tux?"

"You bet." Carolyn felt a delicious swell of tingles as she recalled Allison adjusting the jacket as she stood in front of the mirror. "It's also back in fashion."

The lights went down for the entrance of the concertmaster. Carolyn looked over her shoulder and was relieved to see Alison slipping through the curtain behind the box. She was in her chair in time to join the welcoming applause.

"Phew. I wasn't the only one running."

Carolyn squeezed Alison's hand. After a brief minute of orchestra-wide tuning, the lights were dimmed the rest of the way and Nick entered, smiling. The severity of her crisply tailored tuxedo was softened by a wide smile and a graceful nod of her head acknowledging an enthusiastic burst of applause. She stepped up to the podium and immediately gestured with her expressive left hand for silence. She was obeyed.

With no signal other than her bowed head, a voice rang out, reminding Carolyn both of the Islamic call to prayer and an African chant, though she couldn't discern what language it was. She let go of her vexation that she'd not been early enough to study the program and gave herself over to the music.

They were so close to the stage she could easily spot the tenor who was singing. Moments later, she was swept up in the motion of the cellos as they softly began an accompanying harmonic drone. The call was repeated twice more. In the universal language of music, they were clearly being called to join together.

The tenor finished and Nick raised her head. Her right arm signaled more volume from the cellos as the violins and violas quietly merged into the rising hum and the drone took on a melodic form. After a moment, Carolyn realized it was "Gabriel's Message." Not in the style of the Basque hymn—it was much closer to Sting's understated arrangement. Leave it to Nick to mix traditional and modern into something new.

After that, if the piece was unfamiliar she watched the musicians. If she knew it well, she watched Nick. It was a marvel how a minute lift of her right hand brought a ripple of response in anticipation of a time change. How the left hand coiled and relaxed and her long fingers pinched and spread the air. The way she rocked forward and back on her feet as if she braced to lift up the players to the heavens or ease them back down to Earth.

She couldn't recall ever being seated so far to Nick's left that she could watch the expressions on Nick's face change throughout a piece. Her brow furrowed, and her lips pressed into a hard, thin line of concentration. Eyes widened at a sudden shift in tone or pitch, or they closed briefly when the sopranos soared. All of that eased away into the briefest moment of pure contentment as the final note died away.

Toward the end of the night, a sitar virtuoso and several handpan players joined the orchestra. They led the way into a rhythmic raga that was picked up by the big kettle drums in the timpani section. The steady, catchy syncopation was reinforced by the stringed instruments plucking on the downbeat. Everyone else, including the choir, was quickly clapping in a complex counter-rhythm.

To her surprise, the choir gustily sang out "Dashing through the snow" and repeated the line. For a moment it was pure chaos, but a wizard-like twist of Nick's left hand drew the rhythms into alignment. She, Alison, and Margot attempted the clapping pattern. Even her staid, traditionalist brother was bobbing his head with a smile. Below them in the aisles, kids were swaying and twirling.

Celebration. Community. At times like these Carolyn believed the human race could survive itself. Music. Dancing. Her heart full, she wished the whole world could feel this magic.

It was enough, in the moment, to know that those she loved did.

Most of all, Carolyn would never forget—never, ever—the sight of Nicola Frost grinning from the podium like a divine messenger of almighty music as she spread both arms to her sides and danced.

And Now for the Sprinkles on Top

Did I give that secondary character's ex-girlfriend a name? Does this main character have any living family? What color are the love interest's eyes? How tall is anybody? What time of year is this novel? What's the name of the college, sibling, pet, third grade teacher…?

These questions, and ever so many more like them, accompanied my journey through novels and short stories written over thirty-odd years as I prepared this collection. It's a rewarding journey, don't get me wrong. In with the mistakes, missed opportunities, and so many sentences that could have been written more tightly are the sparkles all writers look for—the phrase, or sentence, or maybe even an entire paragraph, where we can honestly say to ourselves and anyone else who will listen, "That's pretty decent, that bit right there."

Speaking of something far better than "pretty decent," I have been blessed with the talents of so many fabulous editors over the years. Katherine V. Forrest's mentorship in my early days and her wise, precise editing in latter ones, comes first to mind. Medora MacDougall brings so much wit and humor to every project that it's delightful to make mistakes so I get more interaction. (I'm not sure she would see it that way.) Heather Flournoy expects me to be able to explain when I deviate from accepted styles and won't accept, "Because it sounds right to me?" This challenges me in all the good ways my aging brain needs.

Speaking of challenges—yes, this collection was due out more than two years ago. For those who don't follow my blog, the first delay was breast cancer (now cured) and the brain fog of post-treatment medication. Life had nearly settled back to normal when devoting a lot of time to my elderly, formerly independent parents became a necessity. Just as that process became more predictable, my father passed away suddenly at 91, leaving my mother's care and the selling of their house foremost in my priorities for much of 2024. (She's fine, we're fine.) There was another brief pause to everything because my elder son got married! A joy after a lot of not joy.

Having been away from the keyboard and my entire creative process for months—years—it took some time to get the writing muscles back online, as it were. I finally made it, much to the relief of the very patient and understanding staff at Bella Books. As I've learned over and over, I am wealthy in the love, respect, and support of colleagues, readers, friends, and family.

* * *

The previous two *Frosting* collections each included my commentary about the conception and writing of all the novels published since the previous collection. *Frosting on the Cake 2: Second Helpings* was published in 2010. Continuing with tradition, here are notes about all the novels since then, plus a few asides about the short stories in this collection.

Roller Coaster

What if a single conversation with a stranger changed the course of your life? That was the idea that became *Roller Coaster*. Then the real work began. How long after this conversation does the story start? (It ended up being 23 years.) Should I put the conversation in a prologue? Or handle it as a flashback so the book begins in the present day? (After agonizing for weeks, I went with a prologue.) More importantly, what paths were these two women already on (chef, Broadway actress) before they met on a roller coaster (that got stuck) and shared their dreams?

These are the fun steps of creating a story. Ideas pour out like pieces of a new puzzle, and I get to assemble them without knowing what the picture is, and besides, the final picture will be different from what I thought anyway. Which is *crazy* if I think about it, so I try not to. But I will say that it's vexing when a little 500-piece puzzle seems so doable, and then it turns into a 5000-piecer, 100 extra pieces at a time, but ultimately it's a 4000-piecer because of what was never in the picture to begin with that I blithely wrote anyway.

Yes, I do this writing thing voluntarily.

Roller Coaster and *Simply the Best* are not linked in the novels, but when I needed a summer escape from Manhattan for Helen and Laura, I decided not to create another interview diva who lived in the Hamptons, not when I already had one in Barbara Paul Cabot.

One last little thing. When I wrote the book, "roller coaster" was two words. For that matter, so was "car pool" in 1993. A writer could take this personally, Merriam-Webster.

Love by the Numbers

Smart is sexy, it absolutely is. I fell hard for my data-crunching professor and her brain, but, wow, she was an ice queen and a bit of a bully at first, which I didn't care for. So who or what was going to help her change into someone worthy of a happy ever after?

Most of my novel plotting starts with this question. For *Love by the Numbers*, the who had to be the *perfect* fit to balance out someone who's very hard to like at the start. For this novel, it came in a ball-of-fire woman who'd been kicked hard in the teeth and still kept smiling. So sunny. Such a morning person. So bubbly, even before anyone has had coffee.

Cackling with evil glee, I thought, "How about I put them on a long, long road trip? This'll be fun!"

And it was. Because smart is sexy, and there is more than one way to be smart.

Captain of Industry

Jennifer Lamont was a straight-up villain in *Stepping Stone*. A wrecking ball, unscrupulous, and willing to grind a stiletto heel into anyone and anything in the way of her ambition. After I finished *Stepping Stone*, I thought I was done with her.

I was wrong. She crept back into my brain and asked, "Didn't you ever wonder what choices and sacrifices and disappointments happened to make me believe I had to be that way to survive in Hollywood?"

I hadn't actually. And then I did. For years before and years after *Stepping Stone*, I explored Jennifer Lamont's life and the "fourth time's the charm" romance a woman that epic deserves. It's a reader favorite, and I think it's because she is, and always will be, an extraordinary thing.

The opening chapter of *Captain of Industry* features a very swanky party in Southern California. I took advantage of the locale to bring together characters from other books (*Wild Things, Just Like That, Painted Moon,* and *Roller Coaster*), threading together the lives of remarkable women who would, in a perfect world, of course know each other.

My Lady Lipstick

My Lady Lipstick is one of the most farcical and fun books I've ever written, if I say so myself. An improbable actress meets a reclusive brownie-baking author who is offered the biggest break of her career. But the author doesn't want to win by lying. That's wrong and absurd. Isn't it?

Isn't it?

It took you too long to answer! And while you were dithering, the actress did it anyway, and, by the way, she steals things.

This novel also includes a reappearance of the irrepressible Lisa from *Warming Trend*. Lisa gets her own short story in this collection, one that ties to both of these novels. Because of course she does, it makes perfect sense, just ask her.

Because I Said So

Don't you hate it when someone says that? I do! But I'm a parent and sometimes that's the bottom line when the young people won't listen to you trying to keep them safe. This novel began with a conflict between sisters. It also has my favorite plot twist, and I thought of it all by my ownself, yes, I did. It popped into my brain, and I literally laughed out loud. The best part is I didn't know the twist was coming until a few sentences from the plot point where it happened. The light bulb went off and boom, I was revising from the start before I wrote another sentence forward.

It was a lot like getting seventy-five percent through writing *Just Like That* and thinking, "Am I rewriting *Pride and Prejudice*?" The answer was not yes, but it wasn't no either, and I decided to make it yes, one hundred percent yes.

Same thing here. Did I want to make the reader get to the end of Chapter 8, shout, "No way!" and then go back to the beginning to make sure? Yes, one hundred percent yes.

Simply the Best

The year was 2020. Yeah, *that* 2020. Not only were we all engulfed in a global pandemic with a rising death toll, we were also simultaneously discovering that all the norms we took for granted could be shattered. That a neighbor would cough in our face because they knew better than the experts trying to keep us alive. That a president would also ignore those experts and then lie about the numbers of the dead.

Simply the Best is the first time I wrote a novel in the near future. I didn't know what that future would be, but vaccines had arrived and there was a path forward. For the characters the pandemic is mostly behind them. The reckoning of the losses is only beginning. They daily confront the loss of friends and colleagues and the pang of funerals never held.

As they try to get out of the despair of all that, somehow they have to find hope in a future when so many people proved, time and again, they would sacrifice everyone else before they'd accept the minor inconvenience of wearing a mask. For my science journalist (smart = sexy, remember?), there's also the rampant selfishness of people always at the front of the line to take and not even in the line when it's time to give.

As you can probably tell, I had some grief to work through. I'll admit I did it in this story, and I even wrote what I think is one of the curse-wordiest, funniest paragraphs I've ever strung together. Because sometimes we have no fucks left to give the villains in this world.

As I discuss further on, we're right back in the Land of Disbelief today. Right before election day 2024 I got out this novel and went to the page where my science journalist finds her hope again, as well as the courage it takes to commit to someone else in a world still on fire.

The day after the election, I went back one more time. I probably will again.

Frosting on the Cake 3: Still Crazy After All These Years

As I said at the top, to write these stories I had to worry about continuity. I reread all of the novels more than once. I opened them all at least a dozen times while first drafting to check the smallest of details. I discovered that at least once I had *never given the character an eye color*. Seriously, Karin? Seriously?

There was also a matter of tone and each character's voice being present in the new story. Oh, and did I mention that some of the novels already had a short story or two inspired by them? Those are also part of the continuity canon.

I hear the characters' voices in my head as I'm writing or editing, so it got really loud toward the end of the project. Thirteen novels that themselves span thirty years of history, with twenty-six characters—one of whom is Lisa, who loves to talk to me, while another is Sabrina, who really doesn't.

All I can say is that I have cleverly on purpose with full aforethought hidden at least three continuity errors somewhere in *Frosting 3*, yes, I did. To the reader who finds all three: I've got a gift for you. I don't know what it is, but it'll be something.

Before I wrap up, I have a few additional notes about a couple of the short stories.

Painted Moon: "Living Canvas" picks up directly after the first chapter events of *Captain of Industry*. It was written for the *Painted Moon 25th Anniversary Edition* released in 2019. I realized that those early readers who had the original Naiad Press edition might have missed out on the Anniversary Edition's bonus content. I very much wanted them—especially them—to have access to this story as well. I still believe in its inherent hope in the generations to come, even after the world-shaking and rebuilding events that have happened since. It has been lightly edited because I can't help myself.

Maybe Next Time: One of the musical pieces mentioned in "Turtles, Adagio" is "On the Nature of Daylight." It was composed by Max Richter in 2003 and first recorded in 2004. If you pay attention to musical scores, you've likely heard this piece used in *Arrival* and *Stranger than Fiction*, as well as in *The Handmaid's Tale* and *The Last of Us* series and many more.

Iz's (Israel Kamakawiwo'ole) mix of "Somewhere over the Rainbow" with "What a Wonderful World" is widely known, and he was the inspiration for the gentle giant who blessed a very young Sabrina.

This is the first time since writing *Maybe Next Time* in 2002/2003 that Sabrina Starling has shown up with a story to tell. Ultimately, she said she simply wanted everyone to know she was okay. Mahalo.

* * *

As I finished writing these stories, after all the delays, election day 2024 happened. Here we are again with darkness our old friend. Does it feel like 1990, 2000, or 2016? For me, it was 2008 when my fellow Californians voted in the first Black president and cheered the huge step forward—and simultaneously enshrined a ban on same-sex marriage. Fellow travelers in the struggle for equality should have had my back—and they didn't.

To someone younger than I am, the past ten years must feel like two steps forward, three steps back.

Yet we are so many steps forward of where we were when I was a deeply closeted twenty-six-year-old lesbian who wanted to write romance novels and then discovered ones for women like her existed.

Over the years I've learned that anger is a useful tool, but it has to have a useful outlet, or it burns you instead. The challenge is to find that useful purpose for it—and to do that while keeping faith with our community and allies and our companions of life.

Hardest of all, we must wield the necessary power of kindness. As I wrote in *Simply the Best*, love is what saves us from ourselves. All kinds of love, which is what kindness represents in the smallest of choices.

Maybe, as I look back over the years, I shouldn't have ever thought the fight for life, love, and freedom would be finished. But I still believe it will be. Someday, not today and probably not this decade or the next, we'll get to take a rest. I'm still that crazy after all these years.

I ended the first two volumes with these sentiments, and they are still true: *I am a lucky woman, and I have all of you to thank.*

Bella Books
Happy Endings Live Here
P.O. Box 10543
Tallahassee, FL 32302
Phone: (800) 729-4992
www.BellaBooks.com

More Titles from Bella Books

Jones – Gerri Hill
978-1-64247-598-2 | 260 pages | Mystery
One weekend getaway, six friends, and a deadly secret that will wash away everything they thought they knew.

Merry Weihnachten – E. J. Noyes
978-1-64247-610-1 | 292 pages | Romance
Christmas traditions aren't the only things getting mixed up when these two hearts collide beneath the mistletoe.

Sweet Home Alabarden Park – TJ O'Shea
978-1-64247-570-8 | 362 pages | Romance
She came to restore a royal estate—she never expected to rebuild her heart.

Dr. Margaret Morgan – Christy Hadfield
978-1-64247-628-6 | 286 pages | Romance
Facing the professor on campus everyone hates is terrifying—but falling for her might be even worse.

Overtime – Tracey Richardson
978-1-64247-630-9 | 278 pages | Romance
A charming romance about second chances, found family, and scoring the goal that matters most.

The Big Guilt – Renée J. Lukas
978-1-64247-657-6 | 206 pages | Romance
What if the one who got away became the one you can't have?